Enemy at the corral gate . . .

"Who—who is out there?" she shrieked.

Slocum threw back the covers and the cool air of the cabin's interior swept his skin as he jumped up. She stood in the open doorway. He grabbed his Colt, shucking the holster en route to join her.

Slocum saw a buck with war paint on a piebald pony at the corral gate. "No, you don't!" he shouted.

The revolver bucked in his hand. Off-handed, he realized it missed his target. He took aim as the Indian quickly turned his horse around. Obviously unscathed and screaming like a coyote, he ducked around the corral, spoiling Slocum's second chance for another shot at him.

He watched the intruder at a dead run climbing the slope through the junipers. No sense wasting ammo; he was beyond any pistol shot. Nervy outfit coming back. Slocum exhaled out his nose.

"Who!? Who was he?" Her voice quaked with fear.

"One of them," he said. He hugged her shoulder. "He can't hurt you."

JAKE LOGAN

SLOCUM'S WARPATH

JOVE BOOKS, NEW YORK

SLOCUM'S WARPATH

A Jove Book / published by arrangement with
the author

PRINTING HISTORY
Jove edition / February 2002

Visit our website at
www.penguinputnam.com

ISBN: 0-515-13251-9

A JOVE BOOK®
Jove Books are published by The Berkley Publishing Group,
a division of Penguin Putnam Inc.,
375 Hudson Street, New York, New York 10014.
JOVE and the "J" design
are trademarks belonging to Penguin Putnam Inc.

PRINTED IN THE UNITED STATES OF AMERICA

10 9 8 7 6 5 4 3 2 1

Chapter 1

In a long trot, he pushed the dun horse, Buddy, off the mountain slope. Against the warm afternoon sunlight, his eyes narrowed on the towering black streak in the sky. That smoke meant more than a cooking fire in a chimney—someone's place must be ablaze for that much of a mark. Word back in Colorado was that several bands of the Jicarilla Apaches were on the warpath. Another reason why he'd used this lesser-traveled trail making his way down through northern New Mexico.

The black thread niggled his conscience until he turned the dun in a more easterly direction to swing close by for a look. If the cause of that streak had been an Indian raid, he'd probably be too late to do much good for the victims, but still he needed to check it out. However, he had no intentions of running head-on into a pack of bloodthirsty young bucks. He reined the gelding around a large juniper, and once clear he tried again to see the source of the smoke by standing in the stirrups.

No such luck—he'd have to get closer. The ring of the pony's shoes on the rocks sounded bell-like. He undid the leather tie-down loop on his Colt. More than likely by this time the attackers were long gone, but still it paid to be careful.

When he reached the next point, he could see the blackened ashes of the fallen-in roof, the log walls still blazing.

1

Too late. He checked the dun, his other hand on the gun butt, and surveyed things. There was a body on the ground between the corrals and the burning house. Been pretty tough down there. Apaches never left things nice after a raid. He tried to steel himself for what he would find. With no sign of a living thing, he booted the horse on.

On his approach, he searched around, trying to listen for any telltale sounds above the crackle of the fire. Then, still wary, he dismounted beside the body of a woman. The bloody gash in her head made him shudder. Her blue checkered dress had been ripped open, exposing a pear-shaped breast. The stark whiteness of her skin was smudged by dirty handprints where some attacker had fondled her.

She groaned. He blinked at her. She was still alive, to his amazement. He quickly checked around to be certain they were alone, then dropped to his knees beside her. She made another toss of her head when he picked her up to examine her wound. With care, he used his fingers to move the hair back from her face. Her eyes opened, then widened at the sight of him. She drew a deep breath of fear up her nose.

"I'm a friend," he said. "They're gone." What could he do for her? He spotted a small log building. It could have been the *first* cabin on the place. The door stood open. Perhaps he could find a place for her inside there.

"Who did this to you?" Slocum asked, shifting the weight of her body in his arms as he picked her up. Dried blood covered half of her face from the deep gash that still wept crimson fluid over the crusted portion. Her dress was torn and filthy with dirt. No telling how many savages had attacked her. He guessed her to be in her mid-twenties. Long strands of tousled black hair obscured her face, but her beauty was not to be denied by the grimness of her pale complexion.

". . . Val . . ."

"Val who?" He ducked under the low doorway and checked around the rampaged interior of the feed-smelling room. Those bucks sure made a big mess of the place. Stepping over things dumped on the floor, he carried her limp form to a canvas cot against the wall. With care, he laid her down, then swept some of the hair from her face. Her eyes were shut. On his knees beside her in the shed's shadowy interior, he wondered what he could do next for her comfort.

Her eyelids flew open. The pupils widened in fear and she began to scream at the sight of him. Terror filled, she tried to raise and escape, but he caught her shoulders and held her down.

"Easy. Easy. It wasn't me that done this to you, lady."

Her screaming grew louder. His efforts to contain her for her own safety required more force. He realized the wild look she gave him was not focused, nor was the strange shape of her mouth right either. Dumbfounded by his discovery that she'd slipped away from sanity, he struggled harder to contain her on the cot.

Her flailing arms and legs joined in the melee. As she kicked and swung at him, he wished for more help. The insistent cries escaping her throat hurt his eardrums. Her resistance grew to superhuman proportions and only by gritting his teeth and using all his force could he keep her down.

Where was a rope? He tried to search around and at the same time fought to control her. Then at last, she went limp on him and fainted. He dropped back in relief and mopped his sweaty face on his sleeve. His breath raged through his throat. Who was she? Where were her people—husband—family?

Shaken by the turn of events, he rose to his feet, staring in disbelief at her disheveled form. He didn't even know her name. Long, shapely legs, completely exposed from her thrashing, were floured with dust—a sign for him that her attackers had struggled with her in the dirt outside where he found her. For her own safety, he needed to tie her down to the bed. If he didn't, when she awoke there was no telling what she might try to do. While the notion of binding her bothered him, he could think of nothing else he could do. Perhaps after she was tied, he could clean up the deep cut on her forehead and stem the bleeding. The notion of his responsibility to her weighed heavy on his mind. She needed medical attention—he'd have to do the best he could for her.

On a wall peg he found some cotton rope and soon bound her hands to the side of the cot frame. As he tied them, he hoped when she awoke she would be back to her senses. No way for him to know how her mental state would be then, but he wanted to clean up the nasty gash on her forehead that ran back into the hairline, and stop the blood that trickled in small streams down the side of her face. No telling where else she was hurt. Before he stood, he restored the dress's bodice to conceal her breasts and the skirt to respectably cover her exposed legs.

He went to the doorway and stared toward the corrals. The gates stood open. Obviously, the raiders had taken any stock in there. No time to worry about that. He recalled a walled-up well in the yard and turned back inside to search around for a pail. An older canvas bucket lay on the floor with the long-handled gourd dipper having been smashed under someone's foot in the rape of her shed.

From the well, with the acrid stink of the cabin's fire in his nose, he could see across the sagebrush sea for miles. Far to the east rose the sacred mountain of the Taos Pueblos. He removed the cover and dropped the pail. It splashed in the watery depth and he fished it with the rope to tip over and fill. Soon, the weight told him it was full. With his gaze to the north, hand over hand he drew the pail up. In deep concentration, he studied the tablelands that her place rested upon and looked toward the lofty, far-off heights that rose into the Colorado San Juan range.

The dripping bucket set aside, he replaced the board lid. It was a pretty place, set back in the junipers at the base of a mountain. He shook his head. By herself, she couldn't be running a cow outfit on the western side of the Rio Grande Gorge. He decided the water container could sit there for a moment while he went around the shed to search for more answers.

Out in back, a small flock of brown chickens scratched about and ignored him. The gate of the coyote-proof fence stood open. He walked over and looked inside the pen. Crumpled on the ground lay a man on his back with his boots and spurs set apart. His red underwear shirtfront was black with dried blood and his eyes stared at the azure sky—forever. Perhaps thirty years old, the white man had a pale forehead from years of wearing a hat, and a bushy brown mustache that matched the leathery color of the rest of his face.

Someone had stolen his kerchief or he had not been wearing it, for his neck too was bone white. Slocum squatted down and carefully reached out to close his eyelids. There were three bullet holes in his chest, and any one of them would have killed him. Fired at such close range, they burned some of the underwear material around the tar-black wounds. He never suffered.

A few noisy ravens swept by overhead and nosily scolded him as he rose to his feet. This dead cowboy presented more problems for a man drifting south out of Colorado on his way to nowhere. He'd stepped into a hornet's nest when he swung by this place looking for the source of smoke. A woman gone off the deep end inside and her man needing burying. He thumbed the Stetson up on his head. Lots of questions to answer here. Not many telltale signs of what band did this. Maybe the dead man had brands on his horses that were gone or taken from the corral. This was a job for the law or the army—if there was any.

He walked back toward the well. He didn't need any worse news. With the pail in his hand, he went to see about her. When had all this happened? Early that morning? The dead man not being completely dressed made him believe the ones responsible had came or had been waiting at dawn. But it appeared to have been well planned: her man somehow was coaxed to the chicken pen in the early hours and then slain there.

Slocum needed to clean and close her wound. Then he must dig a grave for the dead man. Perhaps find some food for the two of them to eat too. He had no idea when she ate last, but his own belly gnawed at his backbone. It had been over a day since he had eaten much more than dried crackers and moldy cheese from his saddlebags.

He set the pail on a crate and glanced in her direction. She had not stirred. Good enough. He went outside to the dun horse standing hipshot and ground tied. From the saddlebag pockets, he removed a brown bottle of whiskey and held it up to the sun to gauge the contents. Half full or at least a third. Best that he saved the contents for treating her wound, rather than taking a deep snort for himself, though the thought of a good swig was tempting as hell.

Also, from the bag, he removed a small packet of catgut and a fishhook needle. Her wound needed closure. The very idea of his handiwork and the bad scar it would leave on her forehead niggled him, but the open gash had to be fixed. Inside, he found a chipped cup to soak his thread and instrument in whiskey. Then, with the wash pan on the box opposite the one he had dragged over to sit upon, he began with the cleanest of petticoat rags he tore from her undergarment to cleanse the area around the wound. Her hair around the site would need to be cut away and the dried blood in it proved hard to remove.

Any moment he expected her to awaken and go back to screaming. He drew back from his cleanup when she spoke.

"That you, Ruff?"

"Yeah," he said, holding the damp rag that he had been using to scrub her forehead. No need to upset her. If she figured he was her man then it might keep her settled while he sewed her up.

"My head sure hurts."

"You know you have a nasty cut?"

"I can feel it too. How come am I tied up?"

"You were pretty delirious a while ago and I was afraid you'd fall off the cot," he said, wondering if she really thought he was Ruff. Was that her man's name? Must be. She didn't seem to recall the attack or whatever else happened earlier.

"What are you doing to me?"

"I've got to stitch up the cut in your forehead." He waited. When she didn't answer, he continued. "It's pretty nasty. Going to hurt some for me to do it."

"I'll be . . . fine." He saw her grip the edge of the cot with her fingers. "I'm not a baby."

"I know. But baby or not," he warned, "this sure isn't going to feel very good."

She closed her eyes. "I'll tough it."

He shrugged. With his razor, he carefully dry-shaved her hair back so the wound area was clear enough for him to sew shut. Nauseated at the thought of his next move, he began to wet the fresh end of the rag with whiskey.

"Hold tight, girl." Gently as possible, he used the cloth to roll out the dried blood and dirt from her wound. She stiffened under his efforts and he drew back to be sure she was all right.

"Go ahead," she said through her gritted teeth.

"I'll hurry," he promised. At last, he felt satisfied that was all he could do to cleanse the site and the deep gash, and he readied himself to begin the stitches. Blood continued to flow from the wound. They spoke about small things. Her chores that needed doing. He assured her the chickens were fine.

"This will hurt," he promised and started the suture process.

He felt her wince as he hooked the needle through both sides and drew the catgut tight at the base of the cut, but she steeled herself. Using his large knife when he had it tied, he cut the threat that drew the edges together. Tough girl, he decided. His fingers trembled as the sharpened needle's end sought its way through the layers of flesh and then reappeared on the far side. With a cringe of his own he drew it up and tied the second one.

"Going to take several more," he warned her.

"I'll make it," she said, and he saw her swallow hard. Beads of sweat popped out on her face.

The job at last was completed. He sat back and considered drinking the rest of the whiskey. With a fresh rag, he dappled at the perspiration on her face, then mopped his own wet face on his upper sleeve. Damn, his black stitches looked crude, but only small droplets of fresh blood wept from the seam. So perhaps his job would work, but the inevitable scar would run out of her hairline several inches down her smooth forehead.

She was lucky to be alive. He considered the rest of the whiskey again. Maybe she would rest some with it in her. Damn, he could hardly figure out what to do next. She thought he was Ruff or said so on the start—even acted like she was satisfied with his identity. Good. He wiped the corners of his mouth on the side of his thumb; the whiskey fumes from the open bottle went up his nose and his teeth felt ready to float away.

"I'll be back," he promised her. In his saddlebags was his tin cup.

He rose wearily, went and found it. Inside again, he splashed four fingers of the liquor in the cup. With a shake of his head to dismiss his deepest concern for her welfare, he went back to her.

"I won't fall out now," she said and indicated her hands.

"No," he agreed, set the cup down and leaned over to undo the ropes. That finished, he straightened. "Sorry if my doctoring hurt you. Here, drink this whiskey," he said as she sat up, rubbing her wrists.

Without a word, she took the cup in both hands and raised it to her lips. Half choking on the first try, she soon had the raw liquor down and wiped her mouth on the back of her hand.

"Tough stuff," she gasped.

He agreed. Still standing over her, he took the empty cup back and wondered what she did and didn't know. Best to make her stay inside, while he dug a grave. Things sure were in a mess.

"Lie back down," he said. "And sleep some more."

"I won't fall out."

"I won't tie you."

She pursed her lips in a kiss for him and then shut her eyes. "Sorry, I'm such a baby."

"No problem. You just rest."

When she lay back down, shut her eyes and turned to lie on her good side, he glanced at the log ceiling for some help from above. She still did not realize the fate of her husband. Good. He better take a blanket along to wrap him in and find a shovel. He located an old wagon sheet for a shroud and a good, long-handled shovel. The next task would take hours.

The earth proved unyielding. Gravel and ground were cemented against his best efforts. Until at last, nearing exhaustion, he felt that the waist-deep hole was enough to keep the remains from being dug up by varmints. The sun grew low over the mountains above him. The shovel set aside, he rubbed the dirt from his sore fingers. Then with some effort, he climbed out of the hole.

There was no way to carry the stiff corpse, so he dragged him by the boots from the chicken pen to the grave. At last, with her husband's remains beside his handiwork and him out of breath from the exertion, he paused to rest.

He checked the man's pockets for money and valuables. With care, he placed them on the ground—a jackknife and two agate marbles. Perhaps the killers had taken all of his money. He even pulled off the man's boots in case he had some money secreted there. Nothing. Then at the last moment, he removed the spurs and set them aside. She might want them.

With the corpse finally wrapped and tied in the sheet, he climbed back in the grave to place the body in it. Busy trying to drag the form closer, Slocum looked up and saw her outline standing there against the red flare of the sunset. She wore the old blanket around her shoulders and she hugged her arms close as if she were cold. He had been so heated up from working he had not considered it cold or even cool. Then the juniper-scented wind swept his face and a chill ran up his spine through the icy beads of perspiration on his back.

"That's one of them who raped me, Ruff?" she asked.

For a long moment, Slocum's mind froze, then he nodded. For her sake, he would lie. For the straight-backed lady whose mind danced in and out of such a fragile reality, he wanted to be gentle. She could learn the truth later when he could place her amongst comforting friends or relatives; for the moment, she deserved some pampering on his part. What else could he do?

"That sumbitch!" she swore and turned on her heels. "I'll fix us some supper."

"I'll be there," he said after her and climbed out of the hole. His back complained as he bent over to begin filling in the grave. *Lord, receive this man. He would have given his life for her and perhaps he did. Hold him in your hand, Lord.* Slocum felt a knot threaten to cut off his breathing. He kept tossing dirt and rocks that clanged on the shovel into the hole until, at last finished, he straightened and in the growing twilight could make out the red glow of the burning cabin's walls.

Good-bye, Ruff.

Chapter 2

When he came around the shed in the dusky light, he spotted a gray mare drinking at the trough inside the pen. Potbellied, she bore white saddle scars, and though uncertain about her ownership, he still wanted to capture her. They would need her for the woman to ride if they left this place. He moved carefully and soon had the gate shut. Relieved, he drew a deep breath and considered the dun. Better unsaddle and put Buddy up with her. There was some hay in the racks for them; he'd grain the dun too.

"Are you coming?" she called from the doorway.

"In a minute," he promised and led the dun in the pen.

The saddle and pads on the fence, he went in the pole barn. The light from the cabin's fire illuminated the inside, where he found a nose bag and some corn. He went back and fashioned it over the gelding's head. The mare nickered at him, but he shook his head at her. "Next time, girl."

Filled with concern about the woman's mental state, he clapped Buddy on the neck. "I'll be back and take that off." Then he let himself out of the pen. Stars had begun to fleck the clear New Mexico sky. He wiped his whisker-bristled mouth on his calloused palm and wondered about the lamp-lighted doorway and the woman inside. Had she discovered the mess?

He ducked inside and stopped so she would get a good look at him. She turned mildly to nod at him. Most of the upset things in the shed were picked up, and to his relief, she acted settled.

"How's your head?" he asked.

"Sore, dizzy. I'm fine," she said to silence his concern. "But I forgot I had no food—there's a deer carcass hanging in the barn, if they didn't steal it."

He nodded that he heard her. "I'll go see about it. If we have one, I'll cut us off some steaks and build a fire."

She nodded and wrapped the old blanket around her.

"You lie down and rest," he scolded her.

"I could help you—"

"No, lie down, you've done enough work in here." He shook his head, realizing her effort had been herculean to do so much straightening in the shack. When he had her on the cot again, he looked around at her handiwork. The effort showed.

"Couldn't find any—" she protested.

"Never mind, I'll get something to cook it in."

"Sorry, I'm so weak. . . ."

He put the cover over her and went to find the meat. The carcass wrapped in canvas hung in the top of the barn. With a rope and pulley he lowered it and cut some slices off the ham. Satisfied it would be enough, he restored the rest to its place at the peak of the roof. In their haste to steal things, the Indians must never have looked up.

He carried the meat to the shed and put it on top of a crate while he searched for utensils. She was asleep. Good. He went outside to the cabin's glowing fire. The heat scorched his face as he kicked some fiery logs together. With the skillet from his saddlebags placed on them, he soon sizzled the venison. Heating water in a tin can for coffee, he wished for more than one plate, but they could share his.

The meat close to done, he turned it. He added ground coffee to the boiling water and, satisfied with his progress, looked around as she came out to join him. Wrapped in the blanket, she took her place on the ground close to him. Whiffs of smoke from the ashes were swept on the night wind.

In the fire's light, he could see she had scrubbed her face; the dried blood and the rest of the dirt was gone. The strip of hair he shaved away left the wound like a chunk cut out by an axe from fresh wood. Her long, black hair was pulled back behind her head. She still had pride and he always heard that would be a strong route to healing.

"Meat's cooked enough," he said, using his jackknife to fork it out of the pan.

"I sure hate to impose, but I need a bath after supper."

"I can haul up the water for you if there's a tub." Their gazes met and he stared into her eyes and said, "We can use that half barrel I saw in the shed. Won't be any problem."

Without any sign of her seeing him as someone different, she dropped her look from him. Then he noticed she was left-handed when she used his knife to spear a slab of the browned venison. The food tasted good, but still wadded in his mouth as he chewed for a long while on each forkful, wondering when and how she would emerge from this dream world. Would she come out of it screaming or simply turn back to how she was before the attack? Damn, oh damn, he needed to take her to town and find some physician who could help her. This raid needed to be reported to authorities, for it had the implications of more attacks on other innocent people unless the marauders were stopped.

Then he shrugged. What would the thin veil of law up there do anyway? How could he help her? Find her relatives and leave her with them. That might be hard. So many folks' only kin were miles away in the East and in her current mental state, she couldn't tell him who they were.

"You aren't hungry?" she asked, glancing over at him.

"Hungry enough," he said, drawn out of his own reflections.

He ate two more pieces of the meat, then fished in his shirt pocket for the makings. He started to rise to his feet to move off and smoke.

"Smoke here," she said and refilled their coffee cup from the can.

He picked out a paper and added a pinch of tobacco to the V. Then he twisted the cylinder and licked it shut. A torpedo match scratched on his leg and he puffed the cigarette alive.

"That smoke smells good tonight," she said dreamily.

"You want a drag?" he asked, offering her the roll-your-own.

She shook her head with the same bland look on her face. He nodded in approval and drew on it, inhaling the smoke deep in his lungs, hoping the nicotine would settle his ragged nerves. Some easing of his body's tension began to spread through his muscles and he flicked the ashes on the ground. He drew the last hot smoke from it before it burned his fingers and then ground it out in the dirt.

"I'll start getting your water," he said, meeting her look. "It'll sure be cold."

She nodded. "Any water will be fine."

He took the pail and went to the well. Off in the sagebrush flats, a dog coyote yipped at the stars and another replied in a mournful chorus. He brought the sawn-in-half barrel from the shed. The contents of several pails poured in, he looked for her. She was taking off her shoes.

"I'll get some more for you to rinse with," he said.

"If I wasn't so dizzy, I'd do it. . . ."

"No, I can get it for you."

She nodded and began unbuttoning her dress. He dropped the pail down the well for more water. Didn't she know or realize he wasn't her husband? Her undressing made no difference to him as long as she rode the main beam and didn't go screaming off the deep end again. No way he could handle the screaming woman of earlier. He lifted the rinse bucket full, set it aside, then recalled the feed bag was still on Buddy. He excused himself and went to the pen. Forced to slip in the corral, he removed it from Buddy's head under the pearly light of the stars. Then with a clap on the pony's side, he started for the gate; at the sound of a horse's snort, he froze in his tracks. His hand shot for the holster and the .45 on his hip. He used his thumbnail to raise the leather thong off the hammer.

Who was out there?

The mare nickered and he wondered if the unseen animal was loose. He climbed the corral and tried to see a silhouette in the darkness. But the large, black toadstools of junipers must be concealing rider and horse from his view. He slipped through the fence and, running low, headed for the woman, his Colt ready in his fist. He caught her by the waist, realizing her dress was open as his arm encircled the bare skin of her stomach.

"Hush," he said, hustling her inside the shed.

"Who is it?"

His shoulder to the door facing, out of breath, he looked hard into the starry light for a sign of the intruder.

"I can't see them," he whispered. "But I've heard another horse."

"Oh, no—"

He jammed the Colt in his holster and turned to catch her as she began to faint. An arm hooked around her thin waist and her form hard against him, he saved her fall. With her riding on his hip, he stole another look out in the night. Nothing in sight. Then he turned and caught her ripe body against him.

"No, no," she cried.

"You're safe with me."

"No, no . . ."

He cuddled her head to his chest and wanted to swear at the intruder outside to clear out before he killed him. Her body trembled in his embrace and soon her teeth began to chatter. He reached down and swept her up, placed her on the cot and began to cover her with the blankets from his own bedroll.

"Don't leave me," she protested.

"Stay here and be very quiet. I need to see who it is."

His fingers went to her lips, and she clutched them to hold him there. Then, out of impulse, he bent over and kissed her cheek. "Lie still, I will be back for you."

"I will." She finally surrendered and released him.

He slipped through the doorway. In the darkness, he wondered if the prowler could see him. Then, with his gun in hand, he broke from the shed and made a low run for the well, his next place of refuge.

He sat on the ground with his back to the wooden form and caught his breath. His ear turned, he listened for any strange sound on the night wind. Nothing but the rustle of the straggly cottonwoods in the draw. He wiped the perspiration from his mouth on his palm. Where were they? More so, what was their business there?

He peered around the corner and saw a riderless horse. He looked up and saw her come running from the door wrapped in a blanket. On his feet to stop her, he quickly glanced back to see the animal.

"Who is it?" she asked.

"A loose horse is all. Acts like he belongs here," Slocum said, and herded her toward the shed.

She tried to see past him. He sent her inside and then had her close the door. He went to his saddle and took down his riata. He formed a loop and talked softly to the horse. The animal nickered at the others and he tossed the loop. It flew over the animal's ears and he jerked slack quick enough to close it on the horse's throat. Heels sunk in, he held the pony and soon walked up the rope as the horse blew rollers out his nose at him. He was a good, stout roan horse—must be one of their's who got away from his captors and came home. He led him into the corral and turned him in with the others.

Slocum closed the gate. He turned an ear and listened to the cooling night wind. The horses were sorting out some kind of leadership with a few squeals and licks. That settled, there was nothing else out of place. When he started back, he heard the splash of water and could make out her lithe form standing in the half barrel.

"Who's horse?" she asked, cupping water in her hands to wash herself.

"The roan," he said. That seemed to satisfy her. He picked up the feed sack she had brought for a towel. "You're going to freeze out here."

"I needed to clean up."

He took the towel and began to rub it over her smooth skin. His pulse rose and he grew heady in the night wind. She turned to step out and he took her arm to steady her. Then she stood before him in the dim light like a marble statue.

He knew how Adam felt in the Garden of Eden. What had been the forbidden fruit became for him the dearest thing to ever possess. He regretted the three-day beard fringing his mouth, but their lips met with the forces of two locomotives crashing into each other. She melted against him and soon they were removing his clothes in a frenzy. Mouth to mouth, any missing moments their lips were apart by inconvenience had to be restored in a deeper commitment to more.

Soon she pulled him toward the shed. Breathless, at last,

he was atop her on the cot. He found her gates and then plunged deep into her treasures. His brain swirled with wild desire, the euphoria carrying him like surging waves on the ocean, then harder and harder until lightening struck them and they collapsed in a pile of spent fire and numbed passion.

He realized how hard she still clutched him as he emerged from the faint of their finality. Had their fury sent her over the brink again? He hoped the answer was no, but he dared not move for fear she still walked that tightrope and might fall.

Her body quivered under him, then she sighed, gasped for her breath and let go. He eased himself off the top of her. A word that he would be back and he started for the door. Outside in the starlight, the water in her tub was still cold. He stepped in it, forced to draw his knees up, and began to rinse himself off in the chilly liquid.

Soon, wrapped in her blanket, she joined him. Kneeling beside the tub in the night's darkness and using a rag to slide over his skin, her hard breasts flowed over his arms and back. She said nothing and he only hoped she was returning to herself and not off in some other world.

All he could think about was finding her on the ground, her clothes in a mess and dirt all over her. The gash—he shook his head to try and clear the picture of the day.

"Will you hold me tonight?" she asked as he stood up with water sheeting off of him.

"Yes." He took the towel and vigorously dried himself. *But you can't ask me not to make love to you again.*

Chapter 3

"Who—who is out there?" she shrieked.

Slocum threw back the covers and the cool air of the cabin's interior swept his skin as he jumped up. She stood in the open doorway. He grabbed his Colt, shucking the holster en route to join her.

Slocum saw a buck with war paint on a piebald pony at the corral gate. "No, you don't!" he shouted.

The revolver bucked in his hand. Offhanded, he realized it missed his target. He took aim as the Indian quickly turned his horse around, obviously unscathed and screaming like a coyote, to duck around the corral and spoil Slocum's second chance for a shot at him.

Standing naked with the cool mountain air sweeping his skin, he watched the intruder climbing the slope at a dead run through the junipers. No sense wasting ammo since he was beyond any pistol shot. Nervy outfit, coming back. Slocum exhaled out his nose.

"Who!? Who was he?" Her voice quaked with fear.

"One of them," he said and turned her around for the shed. She wore only a blanket. He hugged her shoulder. "He can't hurt you."

"Hurt me?" She looked at him in disbelief. Then shook her head. "Who am I?"

"You're fine," he said and held her face to his shoulder.

17

She twisted loose. "I know you. You're Ruff. But who am I?"

"Julie," he said, making up the first thing came to him.

"Julie? That doesn't sound right."

"Yes, that's who you are." He looked pained at the mountainside clad in junipers. That buck and his gang of horny redskins had done this to her. No doubt when they finished gang-raping her, they thought the blow to her head had killed her. Apaches hated dead bodies and wouldn't hardly touch them; that's why they didn't take Ruff's spurs. When they rode out, they left her and her husband for dead.

"What happened to me?"

"You had a bad blow to the head yesterday."

"Did I fall?"

"I found you in the yard."

"I am so sore I can hardly walk." She pressed her hands to her upper legs.

"Sit down."

"But I need to make breakfast, some coffee." Her words sounded so dreamy. Then she made a sweep with her arm. "This place is a mess. I need to clean it."

"Don't worry about a thing." He needed her stabilized so he could go and check around the place. If he only knew her real name. Damn, oh, damn. "You stay here, I have to go outside and I'll be back."

"Oh, I'm so sorry." She put the back of her hand to her forehead. "But I am so confused and my head hurts."

"I understand. Don't try to do anything until I get back. Sit there and rest."

"I'll try."

"You'll be better in a while." He didn't feel right about leaving her alone, but he needed to do a few things. When she adjusted the blanket to better cover herself, the action comforted him. At least she had some connection with her past.

"I won't be long." He pulled on his pants, hurried outside and went to the corral. Sharp sticks jabbed his bare soles. His back to the shed, he began to piss in the sandy ground close by the fence. Keeping his eyes on the mountain for any sight of the renegade, he knew he must get her to civilization and away from this place. Nothing looked out of place up the juniper-clad slope. Finished, he shook it and put it away, rebuttoning his pants. They needed to make some tracks, if she could ride a horse.

If only he had a buckboard. No sign of one nor the harness. They must have had one? Strange. Indians sure hadn't stolen it. The rig would slow them down and they liked to be more mobile. Oh, well, he'd see about a saddle for her.

He eyed the two horses, the roan and the gray. The mare would be a better bet—she looked and acted broke to death. The roan, he figured, had a buck or two in him. Then he grinned to himself over what he suspected had happened with the roan. He must have outfoxed the Apaches, got away from them and came home. That was why that buck came back, he wanted the big roan and had tracked him all night. Nearly cost him his life.

Slocum went by the barn, sliced off some more steaks from the deer carcass. The meat wouldn't last much longer without colder nights, so he decided to cook up a good amount and they could take that with them to eat on the way. No time to save and jerk the rest; they had better leave the place and head for civilization.

Still enough hot ashes were left at the cabin site to cook on. He set his meat in the skillet to cook, then went back to the shed to put on his boots while she watched him. He explained how he'd cook the venison. She nodded.

"Then we're heading for Espanola," he said.

"What about the cattle?"

"They'll find feed and water by themselves. We can come back when the Apaches are settled down again."

She agreed with a nod.

He held some hope she might mention someone to see or stay with at Espanola. But she never said anything, merely submitted to his plan. He finished putting on his boots and went outside. She went along and filled the tin can with water for coffee and put it on the fire. They sat back to wait for all of it to cook.

He looked over at her. "Think you can ride?"

"Yes."

"Good, that mare acts gentle."

"Goose? She's kind of slow." She smiled and then shrugged.

"I only have one saddle. Buddy's well broke, but I don't figure that roan would do to ride bareback."

She nodded and stared at the still-smoking shambles of the cabin. "I sure wish I had a better dress to wear."

"We'll find you one. I promise."

"Oh," she said with a sigh. "I know we need to save our money for those bulls. You did buy them?"

Slocum nodded. Whatever she meant he had to agree to. Bought some bulls? The man at the chicken coop had to be her husband—wasn't he? Did someone like a hired cowboy live in that shed? She had found a blanket and the cot was in there. The Indians took everything else worth much. He had thought it to be an ex-residence. A shed that was first thrown up to live in until a better one could be built, then used for storage. He needed more answers.

He served the meat when it was cooked and put the rest out to cool so he could stow it in his saddlebags. They shared the coffee cup, and afterward, he went to catch the horses.

She called the mare Goose. She kind of looked like a Canadian water fowl. He wondered how much she knew and wasn't saying. Like why couldn't she recall her own name and still she knew the horse? Strange, but he had no answers. If she knew her own name, was she playing games with him? He drew up the cinch and finished saddling the gray. Then he caught the roan and fashioned a halter on his head. He went back to the shed and found the soft rope he had tied her up with and made a jaw bridle for Buddy. It would have to do, for the Apaches took everything else of value.

She was busy rolling up his bedding and tying it with rawhide thongs. "I'll be ready to go when you are."

"Sure," he said.

"Ruff?" she called out to him.

"Yes?" He turned in the doorway.

"Won't he swear a warrant out for us if we take the roan?"

"He?"

"Milton." She frowned with impatience at him. "You know. My husband."

A knot rose in his throat. She didn't think he was her husband, but her—*lover*?

For a long moment, he thought for an answer. Then he shook his head. "No, he'll think the Apaches got him too."

She nodded as if the words satisfied her. He dried his palm on the front of his canvas pants and went for the horses. What had he gotten himself into?

In a few minutes, he helped her in the saddle, set the stirrups and then he gave her the roan's lead. He bellied up on Buddy and they rode south. The bitter smoke from the last of the cabin burned the inside of his nose. She booted the lazy mare with her heels as if she knew her. He studied her back and wondered. With a shake of his head, he sent Buddy after her and the high-headed roan that she led.

No sign of the Indian buck, but why did the thought of the horse thief still niggle him? Because he knew sometimes Indians became so caught up in their own obsessions, like they must have a horse at any cost including their own lives. Looking over the juniper-studded mountain, he wondered if this one had that same fever. Plus, where was her husband, Milton? Was Ruff in the grave or off somewhere buying bulls? Damn, things sure were unanswered.

Chapter 4

They made camp beside a diamond-clear stream. The warm afternoon sun filtered through the spinning coin–like leaves of the gnarled cottonwood. She quickly removed her dress and shoes. Then, singing some song about a "Blue Girl," she waded naked into the water as if she had no cares. Slocum caught flashes of gold that danced on her white skin as she used hands full of water to rub on her skin. Her beauty caught his breath and reminded him of the falsehood he was under there. Still, she needed him, whether he was Ruff or not. In two more days, they should be close enough to reach Espanola or some settlement on the Rio Grande where there would be help for her.

He gathered armloads of wood for a fire, dumping them in a pile on the sandy ground. She came from the river and he handed her the sack towel. With a shiver, she began to dry herself, and as she bent over with the towel in her hand, she paused to look up at him.

"Where will we go after Espanola?"

He squatted down on his heels to start the fire. "Where would you like to go?"

She straightened, stretched her arms over her head and he drew in a deep breath at the sight of the slim hips, proud breasts and the fine body before him.

"Maybe Texas?"

"What would we do there?" he asked, scratching a match to life and starting some tinder.

"Why, we could buy a ranch," she said, with a tone of affront in her voice at his question.

"Buy a ranch? I have no money." He looked up for her reaction as she drew the tattered dress on her arms, pulled it together in front and began to button it up.

"We'd have to go by and see *him*."

"Him?" He stacked on more sticks and the sharp smoke turned into his face, causing him to duck away.

"My daddy has the money. I told you so."

"Oh, yes."

"Silly, Jim Bob will let you have—I mean me, have the money for us to buy a place."

"Yeah, Jim Bob—"

"Jim Bob Phillips. I swear, Ruff, your memory is worse than mine."

A cold chill ran down the jaw muscles of Slocum's jaw. He knew a Jim Bob Phillips—in west Texas too. She was his daughter? If she was Jim Bob's daughter, he had the money to buy several ranches if he was of a mind to. And she was married to a Milton someone and running off with Ruff, the hired hand. She claimed she thought he was Ruff, anyway. Whew, did he have a mess on his hands.

"Wish I could remember more," she said, plopping down beside him.

"It'll come to you in a few days."

"My own name—Julie—doesn't even sound right."

He glanced over at her head and the stitches. Swollen some, but no sign of an infection like red streaks or bad swelling. Perhaps his whiskey helped clean it. He sure hoped so.

"We can go by Tatum's Store tomorrow," she announced. "They might give us some food."

"We'll need some by then," he agreed, hoping she knew where this Tatum place was located. He would have to play it by ear. Second, how could he hide his identity from them? They'd sure recognize Ruff on sight and know in minute he wasn't him.

He was damned if he did or damned if he didn't. They would need something to eat by then. In his plans, he hoped to find some isolated store or trading post to stop off and get enough food to get them to town. Then he could—

"I think that Injun's back," she said in small voice and clutched his left arm.

"Where?"

"Down by the river. I saw him on the far bank."

Slocum tried to see where she pointed. The reflection off the water caused a blinding glare that made it hard for him to see the willows. He undid her fingers from his arm with a "stay here."

"Where—"

No time to answer her, he bolted to his feet with the Colt in his fist and ran on his stilted boot heels through the sand in the direction that she first saw the buck. Something moved across the stream and he took a wing shot. That was enough—the buck piled on his pony and rode hell bent for the trees. Slocum paused to catch his breath and shot again at his retreating form, though he knew the range was too far. Ki-yacking like a coyote, the Apache rode over the rise.

"Who was it?"

"That damn horse thief wants the roan, I guess." He ejected the empties and reloaded his pistol from the belt ammunition.

"My, my, he's a persistent sumbitch, ain't he?" She hung a hand on his shoulder and shook her head. "You think he was one of them burned the cabin?"

"I thought so."

"How many were there?"

"I don't know," Slocum said, wondering where she was leading him.

She shrugged and closed her eyes. "I guess sooner or later you'll shoot him, if he keeps coming around."

"If I had a rifle he'd of already been dead."

"Guess the rifles burned up in the cabin." She looked off toward the mountains and nodded to herself.

He agreed.

They ate the leftover cooked venison and boiled some coffee. Slocum wondered if the buck would return that night. Perhaps he needed to keep on guard all night and be sure they had saddle stock in the morning. He looked up the valley and saw no sign of the horse thief.

"I been thinking," she said.

"Yes?"

"We can go by Tatum's Store at Pineyon Flat, get us some grub and then ride like hell for Texas." A big smile on her face, she swept her hair back and grasped a handful, making it into a twist over her shoulder. "We can get to west Texas in three weeks."

"First we better find that store."

"Tomorrow. Tomorrow," she said and looking at the purple sky began singing some song about "Adelane."

He tossed some more wood on the fire. Cottonwood wasn't the best firewood, but it beat rocks and that was all else that he could find. Apaches hated night, a fact in the growing twilight that settled him some about the persistent buck's actions. If they were killed at night, they never went to heaven, so they usually did little about things after sundown. It was the first peek of dawn they liked to be there for.

"Adelane, Adelane, I know you're there. . . ." she sang.

He rose up and went to bring her to the fire. They had enough cooked meat left for another meal in the morning, then they'd be on their own until they found that store. He guided her back and sat her down. She was still singing absently.

Before daybreak, he had the animals saddled. With her wrapped in one of his blankets for a coat, they set out southerly. In the purple light that invades the predawn, riding along, he felt several times for the Colt. Her ahead and leading the frisky roan, he continually scoured the shadowy land around them for any sign. Soon they were up on top of a sagebrush mesa and he felt better. But the threat of the horse-stealing buck still needled him sharply.

Near noon time, he drew up and studied the pens and smoke coming from the chimney of the store. Horses and stock about the place looked natural enough. He nodded to her it was okay to continue and they began the long descent to the trading outpost. She was singing about "Blue Girl" and riding ahead of him. He pushed himself off the top of Buddy's withers and seated himself further back as the steep way off the mountain had slid him forward.

It was then he saw them. Several bucks in war paint on

horseback were pushing off the ridge to the south and they too were headed for the store.

"Ride!" he shouted at her. "Turn that damn roan loose."

She put her heels to the gray, but never released the lead. He drew his pistol and began firing it in the air to warn the folks below. Two men rushed outside armed with rifles and quickly looking around to see about the shooting. They began making smoke out the ends of their barrels at the Indians.

Slocum holstered his revolver and sent Buddy downhill. One of the men caught her gray and she leaped off, still holding the roan by the lead. Slocum joined them, took the lead and tossed his head for her to go toward the store.

"Thank God you saw them and warned us with your shots," the older, gray, bearded man said, still looking for sight of the Apaches who had melted away.

"They ain't through yet," Slocum said, taking the leads to all three horses and heading them toward the corral.

"That's Mrs. Combs, isn't it? Guess Milt's gone off on business, ain't he?" the younger one asked, jamming fresh cartridges in his Winchester.

"They attacked her place, two days ago. Killed a man, guess his name was Ruff. She's out of her head and thinks I'm him."

"Sounds bad. Sid's my name, that's my boy, Hiram." The older man swiftly drew up his rifle and aimed at some target on the mountain side. The rifle roared and Tatum shook his head. "Missed him."

The horses inside the pen, Slocum dropped his saddle and gear on the ground. The two men were still keeping an eye out to cover him.

"So call me Ruff, so we don't upset her," Slocum said as they hurried for the porch.

"We savvy, mister."

"What is her given name?" Slocum asked.

"Dorothy."

"I called her Julie when she didn't know," he said with a wag of his head. "You got an extra rifle?"

"Plenty of them inside," High said. "We'll call you Ruff too and tell the women folks."

Out of breath, the three men stopped on the porch to size up the next action of the Indians. Slocum couldn't see any movement from them, but an occasional sight of a paint pony's butt in the junipers out of rifle range told him enough. They were working up their nerve for an attack. A man had to think like an Indian to know them. A leader would try to whip up enthusiasm to make a charge. Everyone did not have to go on the mission. You weren't criticized for not going with them. Perhaps your medicine was not right or you saw a ghost and it warned you. A witch could tell you to beware of some sign on the trail. But if that leader had enough talking power to convince you, soon you were in a fighting fervor like a religious zealot and not even bullets would stop you.

Slocum knew full well, as he ducked to enter the store, such an impromptu council was in session up on the hillside.

"Good day, sir," a young woman in a freshly starched blue dress addressed him.

"How is Mrs. Combs?" he asked softly, looking about and not seeing any sign of her.

"She's asking for you. My mother-in-law took her in the back to lie down." The woman made a face, glanced around to be certain they were alone. "What happened to her head?"

"Apache hit her."

"Oh, did they try to scalp her too?"

"No, I did that sewing it shut."

The woman hugged her arms to her slender form and shook. Then the sounds of rifle shots on the porch came and he looked around for one.

"Get me a rifle and some ammo. They need me out there."

She rushed over and took a new .44/40 from the rack. He took it and swung down the lever and opened the chamber. Her fingers shook as she dropped brass cartridges in his hand. As he inserted them, he could hear the war cries of the Apaches and the thunder of horses' hooves. His vest pockets crammed full of shells, he nodded at the blanched-faced woman and headed for the front door.

An arrow stuck in the door facing and quivered as he ducked outside. With the rifle butt in his shoulder, he fired at the arrow-shooting buck's brown-skinned back. His shot was true. The Apache threw his muscular arms in the air and cartwheeled off his horse. Slocum swiveled and drew bead on another screaming horseback rider with red and yellow streaks on his face. The rifle cracked and he too flew sideways off his brown-and-white horse, who shied over the top of him and fled bucking past the corrals.

The other two men were busy reloading. The bulk of the Apaches were farther off than the less fortunate two, firing rifles and pistols at them, but the range was too far.

"Bring the Sharp's!" Sid shouted and the young woman appeared in the doorway. The older man took the long gun, put in a cartridge and used the porch post to steady his aim.

About then, an Apache on foot in the line of riders dropped his breechcloth and began to moon them with his bare ass, thinking he was safely beyond their rifle range. Slocum saw the man intently squint and then squeeze. The loud report of the .50 caliber hurt his ears, but the projectile sent the bare-assed buck face down. The three white men on the porch shared a nod of approval over Sid's marksmanship.

For the Apaches, it was the final insult and they swung on their horses and rode away.

"They ain't leaving for good," Sid said and reloaded the Sharp's.

"No, they ain't had enough," Slocum decided.

"Hey, we sure appreciate you warning us. We've been on our guard since they said Two Bears was on the warpath. But they might have cooked our goose if you hadn't seen them coming in and went to shooting."

"We better post a guard on the roof," Slocum said.

Both men agreed and Hiram went for the ladder.

Slocum turned; he heard her screaming. Dorothy Combs. He looked about at the two still Indians on the ground. He'd found allies, but they weren't away from the danger yet. The devils inside her head must be loose again. He shook his head and went inside to see about her.

Chapter 5

She rushed from the back of the store to hug him. "Ruff! Ruff!" she cried.

He nodded to the other two women that it would be all right.

"I'm fine," he said to reassure her. "They've left."

"For good?" She threw her head back and her eyelids were wet with tears.

"I hope."

"We've got to run away."

"Not yet." He worried she might blurt out something that she would regret later when she found her sanity. "We'll leave when it's safe."

"Oh, Ruff, I'm so afraid."

He hugged her protectively and tried to comfort her. Poor woman lost her own identity and was so upset about the Indian attack. What could he do to make her at ease? Nothing, he knew. They better remain there until he felt dead certain that it was safe to continue on for Espanola.

"How long must we stay here?" she whispered.

"Until it's safe."

"Safe!" she said out loud. "It won't ever be safe till them red bastards are all dead!"

"I know," he said softly, trying to calm her.

"You know they raped me?"

"Yes," he said to hush her.

"No! They raped me! All of them!"

"I'm sure theses ladies don't need to hear about it."

"Why not? They ain't ever had that many dicks stuck in them! Sumbitches!"

"Dorothy! Get hold of yourself!"

She blinked at him, but he knew her eyes didn't see him. A filmy glaze covered them in some unfocused form and she began to talk in broken words. "Fucked by—them. All them hard dicks—you don't know—you weren't there! Not one, not two, but all of them!" Her voice was loud and pierced the interior of the store and made both of the women draw back with wary looks at her.

"Dorothy! Dorothy, listen!" Slocum shouted, hoping to break through to her.

"Stuck their dirty dicks in me!"

He swept her up and carried her to the back of the store. She was hitting him with her fist, screaming, "No! No!"

Looking about the room with his impossible load, he spotted a double bed. He finally laid her on the quilt and then caught her waving arms and pressed them down.

She tossed her head and spoke in words that were unattached and made no sense. Then her gaze found his and her mouth closed.

"Better," he said. "Now rest. Don't get up. Close your eyes."

"I can't. They'll rape me."

"No, Dorothy, they'll not bother you I swear."

"Why are you calling me Dorothy, my name's Edith."

"Then, Edith, go to sleep. You are worn out. It was a long ride here."

"That's better. Calvin, don't leave me here."

Calvin? Who in the hell was he? Damn, he'd about grown use to being called Ruff and she had renamed him. He could see the pain behind her pupils, but knew no way to draw it from her scrambled brain. She finally closed her lids and immediately went limp.

Relieved, he stood up and nodded to the concerned-looking woman in the doorway. "She'll be better after she sleeps." He shook his head, uncertain that she would ever be right.

They closed the door and in the store, he drew a deep

breath. "Sorry, but she's been through hell and her mind's slipped."

The gray-headed woman nodded. "I understand. She has suffered much."

"You know of anything we can use to treat her with?" he asked.

"Laudanum might ease her until you can get her to a doctor."

"You have some?"

The woman nodded.

"We may need to try it next time. Usually when she gets some rest, she makes more sense. I think I must have pushed her too much bringing her here."

"We can look in on her for you."

"Thanks. You know I'm not Ruff?"

"Yes, sir. But we understood that you found her."

Slocum rubbed the back of his neck as the younger woman, Jill, joined them.

"It all right outside?" he asked her.

The younger one nodded.

"You know what Ruff looked like?"

"Thirty years old, wore a silk kerchief and had a mustache," answered the gray-haired woman.

Slocum nodded slowly. "The Apaches killed him. I buried him. What does Milton look like?"

"He must be close to forty, Jill?" she asked her daughter-in-law.

"Maybe older," Jill agreed.

"Where's he? She mentioned him buying bulls?"

"He came through here a week ago." Then she looked at Jill. "In the buckboard?"

"Yes, Mother."

"Suppose he's due back?" Slocum asked.

"Sometime," the older woman said with a nod.

Shots broke out and he quickly left them to grab the rifle and rushed to help the pair outside. Sid held up his hand and stopped him.

"Just Hiram shooting at some lookout that snuck downhill to see what we were doing."

"Get him?"

"Naw, but I bet he pissed in his breechcloth," Hiram said from the roof. "I covered him with dirt."

"Good."

"How's Mrs. Combs?"

"No good mentally."

Pained looking, Sid shook his head. "That's the tough part. I knew a woman back in Texas who the Comanches kidnapped and raped. Rangers caught them in three days, rescued her, but she never was right in the head ever again."

"That and the blow to her head. I stitched it shut, but God only knows what I stitched up in it."

"You don't know her husband, do you?"

"No. Your wife told me the man I buried up there was the hired man, Ruff, who she thought I was until a short while ago."

"Milton Combs. I never figured him for much of a rancher. Always dresses up in a suit like a banker. Drove a herd up here three years ago and paid off the hands after they built that cabin for him and her."

"When did Ruff come?"

"Oh, about a spring ago. Somehow I figured he knew them two in Texas. Came by here asking about them. Combs hired him and Ruff pretty well looked after the cattle. Combs, he'd make them trips on business. Figured he was going to Santa Fe for a high time and some gambling."

"Combs has money."

Sid nodded. "Still, I figured it was strange to me for him to leave a young wife alone up there with that young cowboy for a week or so at a time."

Slocum nodded, but never answered the man. Was there some ulterior motive planned by her husband's absence? He couldn't answer the question. She had acted as if she was ready to run off with "Ruff." Of course, if she ran away, then perhaps Milton would have complete control of the cattle and the ranch that her old dad had no doubt sponsored. Whew, this whole thing got more involved as time went on, with him expecting to escape it any minute and only sinking in deeper.

"See anything up there?" Slocum asked Hiram on the roof.

"Nope, I think they rode back up the mountain."

"Come on down," Sid said and shook his head. "Them

damn 'Paches like to attack when they can win."

"We going to bury them two?" Slocum asked.

"We better. They'll sure stink if we don't," the old man agreed with a wry head shake. "Lot of damn work for two worthless, blanket-ass sons a bitches."

"You know them?" Slocum asked.

Both men stopped and Slocum reached down and turned the first one over.

"Paw Paw was his name," Sid said and leaned on the muzzle of his Winchester. "I give him a sack of beans and corn last winter to feed his starving family. That's what I get for my generosity? Arrows in my store like a pin cushion." He kicked the limp Indian's leg. "Son of a bitch!"

Slocum walked over and glanced down at the other dead Apache. "Who's he?"

"Hmm." Sid pulled on his chin whiskers. "That's Two Bear's son, Man of Thunder."

"You feed him too?"

"Nope, that's the biggest troublemaker in New Mexico. You did the whole damn territory a big favor shooting him."

"And incurred the hate of every Jicarilla?"

"Probably, but I think he was the main leader of the renegades."

Slocum looked to the mountain and saw nothing. Hiram brought two shovels.

"You see that Paw Paw?"

"We were talking about him," Sid agreed. "Let's plant them beyond the corral."

They agreed and went around to start digging. The older man saddled a horse and used a rope tied to a saddle horn to drag the two around for the burial. Slocum and Hiram quickly decided a common grave would do for the two of them.

By late afternoon, the two bodies were planted and covered up. Everyone wiped their brows and straightened. Slocum was grateful to have the job completed. He was considering starting an undertaking business in New Mexico. Been there less than a week and all ready had three burials.

"I've got some sipping whiskey in the barn," Sid said with a head toss. Both Hiram and Slocum quickly agreed. They trudged over to the pole barn and he dragged his precious bottle from the hay. The Kentucky bottle and bond drew an impressed nod from Slocum and the men brought out their cups. Slocum went and retrieved his from the saddlebags.

"Here's to more dead Injuns." Sid made the toast. They clunked cups and drank to each others' better health.

The bourbon went down easy and Slocum wondered if his ward had slept off some of her fears. He studied far across the great basin bisected by the Rio Grande Gorge and watched the last of the sun's golden rays on the Taos Pueblos' sacred mountain. In the morning, if there was no sign of the Apaches, he would take her south to some sort of care. If he had to take her clear to Santa Fe, he'd find her help.

"Look at that damn Injun!" Hiram shouted, pointing at a small figure coming out of the junipers.

"Holds it," Sid said, "that's an old squaw."

"What's she want?" Hiram demanded.

"No telling, but she ain't going to harm us," the old man said and started toward her.

"What you want?" he demanded as the out-of-breath woman stood before him, heaving for her wind.

"Me," she pointed to herself, speaking in broken Spanish, "come to warn you. Two Bears come to kill all white man in the morning."

"How many bucks he got?"

"Plenty. More coming. They heap mad you killed—Thunder."

"Tell him, more will die. I have many guns."

"He got new guns."

"Who gave him new guns?" Slocum asked in Spanish, anxious to know how the renegade got more weapons.

"White man meet him today." She waved to the south. "Get plenty new rifles—bullets."

"How did he pay for them?"

"Much gold."

"Where did he get gold?" Slocum asked.

"Mule train." And she made a motion with her hand to the north.

"Why did you come here to tell me that?" Sid asked.

"You give me food. Not bad white man." She shook her shriveled apple–looking face.

"Guess all your charity did help in some ways," Slocum

said in English for the other two's information.

"Yeah," Sid agreed as if considering what he should do next. "You go to the store. They will feed you."

The old woman smiled and nodded her head. "Good white men."

"What now?" Hiram asked.

"Someone better ride for help," Slocum said.

"There should be soldiers at Espanola or close to there."

"If they ain't out riding around," Hiram said in disgust.

"A man rides all night and if he does finds them, he couldn't get back here with troops, say, until past noon tomorrow."

"I figure Hiram and me, along with the women, can hold them off until then. You think you can get by them?"

Slocum considered the big roan horse. He would be a handful, but probably the most powerful horse on the place. Maybe he shouldn't have been so angry at her on the mountain when she didn't let go of him when he told her to do so.

"I hate to leave you with her." He glanced toward the store.

"Nothing we can't handle. We'll barricade things tight and be ready for them. The rest is up to you."

He looked as the roan threw his head up. The short, light-colored mane fanned in the evening breeze. *You better be born of the wind.* Slocum nodded slowlike. "Go grab me some jerky and a few more shells for the Winchester. I'll pile my kack on the red roan horse and we'll see."

Even when he flexed out the riata, he knew that the roan had already sensed something and fled to the back of the pen. He never asked her if the roan had been ridden. She never asked to ride him, though she disliked the lazy Goose. Inside the pen, the rawhide braided lariat sang over his head, once, twice, but the foxy roan ducked the noose. Then on his third toss in the twilight, the rope settled around his slinging head and Slocum jerked the slack tight. Heels set in the ground with both hands on the lariat, he sat back and turned the pony to face him. Then he went up the rope, talking softly to the big gelding blowing rollers out his nose.

At last, with a halter formed from the riata on his head, Hiram delivered him his saddle. He took the pads and exchanged them for the rope. Hiram held the lead and Slocum tossed the blankets on the roan's back. The horse still tried to shy away, but the saddle came next and Slocum moved in talking in a low voice all the time, gathering the front cinch and girting him. Then he did the back one. Soon he had the bits in the roan's mouth and was ready. He gave the reins to Hiram and went for the rifle.

"She still asleep?" Slocum looked off toward the store. No telling what she'd tell them when she woke up.

"So far."

He nodded and swung up in the saddle. The roan made two forward leaps and then gave a hoglike noise out his nose, then buried his head in the sand. He went skyward on steel-spring legs that propelled Slocum high enough to see the whole country. Then the roan broke into crow hops around the corral, scattering the other animals. Slocum gathered up his head and shouted, "Open the gate when I come by."

The pair shouted and beat the roan on the butt with their hats when he came by them and headed south into the growing dusk. It would be a long night, but no doubt the powerful horse underneath him, unless he ran headlong off a bluff, would carry him for miles. Slocum whipped him from side to side with the reins. *Run, you devil!*

Chapter 6

"Wake up!" Slocum shouted at the man sleeping in the hammock. "Where in hell is the army?"

"Emboden."

Slocum looked north, knowing the Rio Grande crossing and stage station up the road. He rushed out in the darkness, stabbed a toe in the stirrup and swung on the lathered roan. He sent the hard-breathing horse northward. The farmland flew by as he raced to find what he hoped would be the savers of the small trading post.

He soon entered the canyon and his horse's hooves echoed above the churning of the Rio Grande under the bank. At last, with the big roan's breath rasping in the pearly light, he could see the ghost white tents set up.

"Halt. Who goes there?" A soldier with a rifle stepped out and challenged him.

"I must see your commander."

"He's asleep."

"Get him up. Two Bears is attacking the trading post on Pineyon Flats at dawn."

"What do you mean?"

"I mean that folks are going to die, if you don't get that commander up and now!"

"Sergeant Bufford, there's a crazy man up here."

"Yeah, well hit him on the gawdamn head and toss him in the river," a sleepy voice replied.

"There's three women and two men going to die if you don't get your ass out of them blankets!"

"What the hell is all the fuss about?" A bear of man in his underwear came roaring out of a tent rubbing his eyes.

"Two Bears and his bucks are going to attack the trading post at Pineyon Flats at sunup."

The man raised up and tried to see Slocum by batting his eyelids.

"Who the hell are you?"

"Slocum's my name. I've been riding all night looking for you guys."

"Gawdamighty man—what time is it?"

"Damned if I know, but they've already killed a cowboy up there and attacked a white woman."

"Oh, sweet Jesus—"

"What is it, Sergeant?"

"A man who says that Two Bears is about to attack a trading post, sir."

The officer came over, buttoning his shirt. "What is it, man?"

"Two Bears has about a dozen or more bucks and he intends to attack the trading post at Pineyon Flat at dawn. Those three women and two men can only hold out so long."

"Sound reveille. We better get mounted and get up there, Sergeant."

"Yes, sir."

"Thanks," Slocum said and began walking his hot horse to cool him. He didn't need the roan to fall down going back. How many hours to dawn? He studied the Big Dipper and guessed three or four. They could be up there by mid-morning if they—the bugler's tattoo on the horn sent scrambling troopers to awareness. Orders flew and the men rushed off to saddle horses.

"We won't be able to pursue the renegades far," the officer said, walking over to speak to him as Slocum paced back and forth with his head-tossing horse.

"We save the folks—that will be enough for me."

"How long did it take you to get here?"

"Six or seven hours, but I made a wide detour thinking you would be more south of here."

"They well armed up there?"

"The men at the fort, yes. I think they can hold them off till you can get there. But it will be close if Two Bears gets anxious and presses them."

"You make contact with any other hostiles coming in?"

"Never saw a thing of any others."

"Good. The men will be mounted in five minutes. Tell my scouts how to get to this place."

"Captain?"

"Yes."

"The squaw that warned us says that Two Bears has some new rifles. Winchesters and ammo."

The man shook his head in the dim light and looked across the silver river. "We had some word that he was dealing for weapons with some gold he stole."

"He must have done it."

"All the more reason to get up there and stop him."

Slocum agreed and kept walking his roan, who was breathing easier.

"That's Tatum's Store?"

"Yes," Slocum told the scout in leather dress who rode up on a stocky buckskin horse. Even in the dark, the short, squat mountain horse looked plenty tough.

"You want to ride with me?"

"Yes," Slocum said, anxious to return.

"Captain Crawley, me and Slocum are going ahead."

"We won't waste any time, Buck," the officer promised.

Slocum swung up on the roan. "Let's ride. See you there, Captain."

The two men tore off into the night. They rode in a hard trot side by side up the starlit wagon road. Slocum knew the night would be long. The powerful roan under him showed no sign of weakening. His sleep-deprived eyes felt gritty as he strained to see the way in the darkness.

The sun peeked over the far range in the east. Noisy ravens sounded like war cries to Slocum as the two men pushed their mounts, both knowing that the Apaches would have already begun their attack on the store. Then they came over the last rise and the distant pop of rifles cracked the air.

"How many are there?" Buck asked, standing in his stirrups.

"Looks like a two dozen or so," Slocum said as they reined up.

From their vantage point, they could see several bucks racing around, screaming and shooting off horseback at the store's structure. Not a very effective way to fire a rifle; nonetheless, any stray bullet could kill. Then a rifle shot from the store dropped an Indian and he sprawled off his mount in the dust.

"How many are up in the timber?" Buck asked.

Slocum shook his head. "Why don't you slip up there behind them?"

"Fine. What do you have planned?"

"I may ride in and help them in the store."

Buck frowned. "That would be pure suicide."

Slocum ignored his comments and looked over their back trail. How far behind them were the captain and his troopers? He glanced over at Buck, then nodded. "I'm going in there."

"Just as well be two fools." Buck jerked his rifle out of the scabbard.

"You don't have to—"

"Hell, I know what I have to do."

Slocum nodded to the man and then sent the roan off the hillside. He held his .45 in his right fist, ready to intercept the first buck in his way. Buck drove his pony in close and they raced for the store.

When the attackers saw the two, they reined up and frowned at one another. The halted Indians made perfect targets for the men inside and two were shot off their horses. The rest decided that things were too hot and raced off giving Slocum and the scout an open field.

"Hold your fire!" Slocum shouted. "Hold your fire!"

They slid their horses to a stop and with their armaments in hand raced for the porch. Hiram held the door open covering their run with his Winchester.

Slocum's boot soles were on the gritty wooden porch when he whirled to look for the enemy. None were in sight, but now the Apaches had four men with rifles to face.

"I figured you was dead," Hiram said, following them inside.

"No such luck," Slocum said and removed his hat to run his fingers through his hair. They were there and the four Tatums looked unscathed.

"Where is she?" her asked, not seeing her.

"Gone," the old man said. "She up and walked away during the night. We couldn't go follow her, less we leave our own."

"The Apaches get her?"

'We ain't certain," Hiram said. "You know how dreamy she acted. Well, she was one minute helping set the table, the next she was gone and I rushed out to see where her tracks went up in the timber."

"Who's she?" Buck asked.

"A white woman, Mrs. Combs, who was attacked by the Apaches five days ago. They killed her hired man and left her—out of her mind. I brought her here, because her husband was gone away on business."

"She went out there. They probably got her."

Slocum nodded.

"Apaches're coming back," the old man shouted and everyone rushed to take their place at a window.

Slocum nodded, in deep concern about her safety. He checked the Winchester's chamber and then levered in a cartridge. The war cries and thunder of hooves grew louder.

"Did you find the army?" Hiram shouted across the room.

"Yeah, they're coming," Slocum said.

"I damn sure hope they hurry," Hiram said and laughed.

With a nod, Slocum agreed. The younger Tatum had not laughed for the fun of it, but rather the pressure of wondering how long they could hold off numbers eight times their own. He raised up and fired four snap shots at the passing bucks. None showed any effect and he dropped down again as the room boiled with the acrid gun smoke.

Where was she? He dreaded the notion she was in their hands. It might be more than her mind could endure and she would never recover to normal. He recalled again the violated woman in Texas, who sat on the porch in a rocker all day and sang lullabies after her abuse.

He had a vivid recollection of the rocker creaking and her little-girl voice singing, "Blue bonnets, blue bonnets. . . ." A grim reminder of the way Dorothy Combs might end up like, if she was even still alive.

Chapter 7

"Army's coming!" old man Tatum shouted.

Slocum rose wearily to his feet. Everyone was unscathed inside the store and he felt relieved as the sound of the bugler's notes filled the air.

"We're saved," his wife said and collapsed on a chair. She swept her unkept hair back and then buried her face in her arms and wept. Sid went to comfort her.

Slocum, Buck and Hiram went out on the porch as the troopers charged off after the Apaches.

"What now?" Buck asked.

"Need to see if we can find her tracks," Slocum offered.

"Oh, by the way, they ran off with your dun horse," Hiram put in, as the three men left the porch to circle around the store building.

"Figures," Slocum said in disgust.

"Ah, the troopers may get him back," Buck said.

The sounds of their shooting died down. Obviously they had either ran some down or let them go. Slocum searched the dirt as they went toward the outhouse. The tracks of the Apaches' horses churned up the ground. A dead pinto lay on his side, the unmistakable red war paint smeared on his sides, the rawhide bridle on his lower jaw. His glass eye stared at the azure sky. The men walked around him.

"Here is where I found her tracks," Hiram said. "She was headed up the mountain."

43

Buck dropped down and then nodded. "She went that way."

"Wonder how far she went?" Slocum asked absently, looking up the pine-clad mountain.

"We can go see," Buck offered.

"Let's try," Slocum said, anxious to learn if he could help her.

"Guys, I better get back to the store," Hiram begged off.

"We understand. You need to be there." Slocum shook the man's hand and started after the buckskin-clad scout.

"She came through here." Buck pointed to some faint traces.

Slocum felt grateful for the man's skills. He would have had to take more effort to read the signs. He looked back and could see the soldiers were regrouping at the store. They continued up the steep stope and rounded a large rock formation. The trail led higher. He felt by this time she was a prisoner of the Jicarillas and Two Bear. No telling. They continued their pursuit.

"Slocum, come here." Buck waved him over. "See these iron shoes. Could be from your horse they stole, but she must have gotten on it without a struggle. Her foot prints disappear."

"Or some buck jerked her up on the horse with him."

Buck agreed with a nod. "They rode off north, whatever happened."

Slocum looked in that direction and then nodded in agreement with the man. The Apaches had her at any rate.

"What now?"

Slocum turned and shrugged. "I'll go look for her. We better get back and get some horses."

"She must mean a lot to you?" Buck asked as they started back.

"She's a human being in trouble."

"I savvy that. She clean out of her head?"

"She was seriously in trouble mentally, because of the raid on the ranch."

"She have a husband?"

"They said she did. He's off and gone on business, I understood."

"Who is she?"

"She told me she was the daughter of a man I once knew in Texas."

Buck slowly nodded his head. "I savvy you've got a cause in her."

"Guess so," Slocum said as they headed around the outhouse and past the dead horse.

"We've captured six braves," the captain said, indicating the half-dozen Apaches under guard beside the corral.

"Anyone asked them about the Combs woman?" Slocum asked.

"No. I just heard about her and what happened."

Slocum strode over and in Spanish addressed the prisoners seated on the ground. "The woman from the ranch. Where is she?"

The bucks, mostly boys in their teens searched each other's faces. Then shook their heads.

"The Apache who wanted the roan horse?" He indicated the gelding standing hipshot in the road, too tired to go anywhere.

"Red Elk." The others nodded.

"Where is he?" Slocum asked.

They shook their heads.

"Was he here for the fight?" Slocum asked.

"Him no fight. Him medicine man," one of the younger ones said in his broken Spanish.

"Was he here?"

They shrugged.

"Did he steal a dun horse?"

Heads shook, they didn't know.

"Who took the dun horse from the pens?"

They acted innocent and turned up dirty palms for him.

"You think this Red Elk stole your dun?" Buck asked under his breath.

"If he did, then he has Dorothy Combs."

"Another reason to go look for him, huh?"

Slocum looked off at the faraway mountains and then nodded. "Reason enough."

"Where does a Jicarilla medicine man go hide?"

"Somewhere up in the Amaryllis Mountains."

"If I wasn't so busy scouting and needing the pay I'd go with you."

"I'll find him."

"You know, Slocum, I'd bet some good money that you do find him."

By late afternoon, the army's supplies caught them. Several wagons of rations, tents, and ammo arrived. Slocum had slept for a few hours, knowing the roan needed some rest too. Since that would be his horse to ride out on, he wanted him in some kind of shape before he pushed on. The delay niggled his conscience over her safety, but it was all he could do. Besides, if Red Elk decided there was no pursuit he might grow lax and that would give Slocum a better chance to overhaul him.

Seated on the front porch in the late evening coolness, sipping on some coffee and trying to come out of his disappointment, Slocum watched a rider coming from the south. A man dressed in a suit. He reined up his lathered horse and quickly swung down. The graying hair and mustache looked almost too well done.

"What's going on here?" he demanded, indicating the army tents and wagons.

"Apaches are on the prowl," Slocum said.

"Have they attacked anyone?"

"Yes, a ranch north of here and they attacked the store this morning."

"My God, man. My wife . . ."

"You Milton Combs?"

"Yes. What's happened to my Dorothy?"

Slocum squinted his eyes and shook his head in dread over what he must tell the man. "Apaches have her."

"Oh, no—the man—"

"Ruff's dead. I buried him five days ago."

"What is the army doing about all this? My wife—Dorothy, are they going to find her?"

"They'll look, but I figure some medicine man called Red Elk has her."

"What are they doing about it?"

"Not much they can do. If he took her to the mountains, he could hide from a hundred companies of troopers."

Combs took off his hat and dropped his gaze to the ground. "I'll offer a reward."

"That won't get her back. Was she ever prone to spells?"

"What do you mean?" Combs scowled at him.

"I hate to be the one to tell you, but either the Apaches' attack has made her slightly out of her head or she had spells before and this made it worse."

"Spells? What do you mean?"

"I mean, was she having mental problems before this happened?"

"No. Definitely not, and I don't appreciate you asking such a question."

"Mr. Combs, you don't have to." Slocum rose and brushed off the seat of his pants. He disliked the man from the moment he got off his horse. And his rearing back at his simple inquiry didn't increase Slocum's desire to even talk to him any longer.

Combs stormed by him and went inside the store. Slocum decided he needed some whiskey to shake the fog from his brain. When he started in the front door, he could hear Combs giving the captain hell in the back of the store where the officer was seated at a small table.

When the older Tatum woman came to wait on Slocum, he ordered a bottle, then dug out some money and she refused to take it.

"Land sakes, you done enough for us." She handed him the bottle and dismissed his effort to pay her with a head shake.

He smiled at her and went outside in the sundown to drink it. He circled around the side of the log structure and sat on a bench. With his jackknife he cut the seal and then he popped the cork. The first swig was raw and set his ears on fire. In the form of a hot flow of lava, it ran down his throat and hit his empty stomach like a bomb exploding. He wanted to forget all about Combs; he wanted to speculate that despite her captivity Dorothy was all right. And he wanted to dismiss the notion that if he did find her she really belonged to that pompous ass inside chewing the captain's ass off.

A few swigs later, he looked up and into the hazel eyes of Combs.

"I understand that you are going to look for my wife." He beat the felt hat against his leg.

Slocum nodded.

"Why?"

" 'Cause someone needs to." If Combs made one derogatory remark, he intended to bust him over the head with the bottle on his hand.

"I must go along too."

"I ain't—"

"I can pay you."

"Money ain't the reason."

"Then let me go along. I need to be certain that she's all right."

All right? Why in hell's name did he leave her up there alone anyway? It didn't add up. Combs must not have been too damned concerned about her safety when he rode off. Now, why was her being safe so important?

"I told you I could pay you—"

Slocum rose, grasped the bottle by the neck. "I'm leaving at first light. You want to go along, you have a pack horse and supplies for a month ready by then. We can't find her in that amount of time, there ain't no hope for her."

"I'll pay you—"

"You heard me. You be ready at sunup."

"I will."

Slocum headed away from the man, not certain that he could even stand his company for that long. He about fell over the dead horse as he struck out for the timber. He intended to finish the bottle in peace and quiet away from Combs. The very notion of the man's presence made his stomach roil. Damn, what had he agreed to? He took another deep draught.

Buck found him later, seated on a flat rock outcropping with his legs dangling over the edge and the scout produced a fresh bottle.

"Figured you'd need this by now." Buck grinned wide.

Slocum held his brown bottle up and studied the remains through the twilight. It was about empty. "I will before long." Then both men laughed.

"You taking Combs along?"

"Yeah," Slocum said with deep sigh. "Figured he could provide the supplies. But I damn sure ain't working for the SOB."

"Don't blame you."

"I asked him if she had any light-headed spells before the attack . . ." Slocum paused, his brain waves slowed by the effect of the alcohol.

"What did he say?"

"Got plumb pissed about me asking. Somehow—I think she might have slipped before the attack."

"What caused that?"

"I ain't certain." Slocum swung his legs and looked off at the shadowy rocks twenty feet beneath him. "But he damn sure is strange acting about the whole thing." He shook his head to try and clear it. "Near as I can tell she was about to run off with Combs' cowboy. Before he got home from the trip."

"You figure that Combs knew that?"

"I ain't certain what he knew. But I guess his reaction to my asking if his wife was teetched before the attack was in character. Nobody likes to let others know a family member has mental problems. They hide it."

"Yeah, they sure do."

"When I was boy in Alabama I knew about a girl like that."

Slocum could picture her. Betsy Jean was her name. Betsy Jean Edwards, the prettiest girl in the county. At sixteen, she was the belle of the balls with the boys and the younger men in the country. Everyone in his age group had an eye for her and most planned to ask for her hand in marriage.

Then thunder struck: two runaway slaves kidnapped her. They hauled her off into the swamps, thinking they could buy their freedom in exchange for her return. Slocum could recall the sheriff, the angry posse members and the blood-hounds. Those dogs' mournful barking in the night. Waist deep in cottonmouth-invested water, he held his squirrel rifle over his head and tried to keep up with the lamps being carried by older men.

It required two days of pursuit. They finally hemmed the pair in a grove of huge oaks draped with Spanish moss. Ahead he could recall the barks of the dogs. They had them. What about Betsy Jean? All through the sloshing chase, he had imagined himself finding her and sweeping her fainted body up in his arms and returning her safely to her tearstained-faced mother. Betsy Jean had to be all right. Not even a crazy runaway slave would dare touch a white girl. Why, that would be worse than anything in this world that they could do. Especially Betsy Jean—why, every man in three counties adored her.

He soon joined the men holding their guns on the two runaways.

"Where's that girl?" Sheriff Horton demanded.

The pair, obviously exhausted, dropped their heads.

"I ain't asking you again. Where is she? You done murdered her?" he shouted, the anger rising inside the man that was the law in the county.

"No," the taller one said. "She back at Whitcher cabin."

"She all right?" Horton demanded.

The man barely nodded, looking with some fear at the posse that encircled him.

"She tied up?"

The younger slave they called Ert nodded.

"You boys rape her?"

"No, sir!"

"I don't believe that!" someone shouted.

"Cut out their balls and hang them!"

"We going to send some men to Whitcher's shack first," Horton said.

Slocum volunteered, he and four other men set out on the run. Whitcher cabin was four miles to the west, but they could use high ground and ran with their rifles in their hands.

"She might be dead," one of the men whispered.

"Them niggers going to wish they never seen her if they raped her," another man said.

Jim Price, a planter in the lead, said over his shoulder, "Save your breath, boys. We need to find her safe."

"Won't never do it," another said and half stumbled over a downed branch.

Slocum's lungs hurt when they reached the clearing and the moss-covered log structure. Jim Price set his rifle beside the doorway and ducked to enter. Slocum was behind him and they both stopped in shock. Betsy Jean laid on the floor, stark naked, and the dried blood on the inside of her legs told them enough.

"Get a blanket to cover her," Jim hissed and then barred the others from coming inside.

Numb struck, Slocum went and took a sweat-smelly blanket from the bed and draped it over her still form. He never missed the tight, pear-shaped breasts or the triangle of black hair as he covered her. But the dried blood on the inside of her legs was the worst part of the whole thing and he feared for a long moment that he would vomit.

When she moaned, he jumped back. On his knees, beside her, Jim Price tried to comfort her.

"Don't hurt me again. . . ." Her sobs filled the cabin.

"Slocum, you go back and tell the sheriff that the worst thing has done happened."

Frozen in his boots, he stood there. His lungs still ached. Then he nodded and ran outside. Grateful for a fresh gulp of air outside the cabin, the other men caught him by the arm and held him.

"They rape her?"

He nodded like a wooden Indian. Then he tore loose and began to run. His knees pumping high in the growing warmth of the day, he raced through the woods. Sawbriars tore at his clothing, but he pressed on. From the high ground he could hear the bellow of a big bull gator in the swamp, but his only thought was telling Sheriff Horton that Betsy Jean had been violated by her kidnappers.

At last, he reached the grove and the sheriff stood up when Slocum made the last steps and halted before him.

"Was Betsy Jean all right?" the man asked

Out of breath, all he could do was shake his head.

"Was she raped?"

His head nod was what his breathless state allowed him. "Got dried blood—all over her legs—"

A roar went up and the posse became an enraged mass. The runaways were pressed to the ground, screaming of their innocence and castrated in the crudest fashion with their privates severed off at the base of the pubic bone. Then ropes were strung over stout oak limbs. Out of Slocum's impaired vision and still without his wind recovered, he watched the two screaming, bloody victims being jerked to their death by strangulation.

Slocum recalled that day. Betsy Jean never recovered her mind. He could recall passing the great family homestead and seeing a face in an upstairs window. Others said she went on wild binges of running about bare-ass naked until she could be captured and restrained.

It was two years later in the army that Slocum listened to two drunken companions in camp one night as they bragged. Mark Green and his cousin Harvard Coin told how they had raped Betsy Jean and no one ever knew that them slaves hadn't done it to her.

"You never?" Slocum said.

"Sure did. Mark popped her cherry and we both took turns screwing her till we couldn't do it anymore."

"We figured she ever got her mind back we'd be in deep trouble," Harvard said, holding the bottle so the firelight glinted off it. "But that little bitch never did. House slaves say if she ain't tied up that she finger fucks herself all the time. I'd like to have some of her right now; teeched or not, she was damn good pussy."

Slocum got up and puked up his guts. Neither one of them boys returned alive from the war.

"Them Tatum women got food fixed for us," Buck said, breaking into his blackest thoughts.

That's the women at the store, Slocum reasoned. Somewhere on the mountain, a wolf howled and he realized it was twilight. A cold shiver ran up his spine; he hoped that Dorothy was all right, wherever she was at.

Chapter 8

In the peach glow of dawn, Slocum saddled the roan. He could see the packed horse and Combs standing beside his mount. Stupid of him to mention taking him along, but they would have supplies, something he would have been hard pressed to muster. Tatum's no doubt would have staked him to some, but this way he didn't need to ask.

"We intend to push north," the captain said, breaking into Slocum's thoughts. "I know who you are going after. I hope you can find her. Most times the squaws kill any white captives when we strike their camp."

Slocum agreed. "I think she might be in the hands of this medicine man and he may not be in their camp. My thoughts are that he may take her to some sacred place with him."

"Why would an Apache do that?"

"She's not in her right mind. Wasn't anyway." Slocum lowered his voice. "The red men think a person that is out of their mind can be good medicine. Something about they live in the other world that Indians want to get into."

The officer frowned. "Combs know about this?"

"I asked him if she had mental problems before the attack."

"What did he say?"

"Got pissed off.

"That's no answer. But he does get pissed off easy."

53

Slocum swung up on the roan and checked him. "He can get pissed on as easy."

"Yes, he could. Be careful, Slocum, and you ever need anything, look me up."

Slocum touched his hat to the man. Combs was already mounted and with Slocum's head toss to start, he set in and followed him.

The iron horse prints were not hard to follow. That bothered Slocum as they climbed into the mountains. Too easy to track. He kept gazing up at the pine-timbered slopes and wondering why their trail was so obvious. He found places where they stopped and then went on. Her smaller shoe prints were in the dust beside Red Elk's. Combs grumbled a lot about his looking things over so thoroughly, but from what Slocum read in them, she was going along with her captor.

Not that he expected anything else, for in her mind-set she might think that Red Elk was Ruff too. No telling. They had a day's head start and only one horse to ride as far as Slocum could tell. He remounted and they pushed up the steep trail, the roan snorting in the dust with his head low, picking the way skyward.

By sundown they topped the pass. A cold wind swept the rocky point where they dismounted and Slocum used his brass telescope to look for signs of the pair. He could see down the side of the yellowstone-lined canyon, with eroded pipes like deep wrinkles in the steep face of the sides. Nothing.

"How far ahead are they?" Combs asked.

"A day or half a day," Slocum said, offering him the glass. Combs shook his head at the offer.

"I say that we push on all night and catch them."

"Or ride right into an ambush."

"Hell, he's just one Indian."

"He ain't that stupid. I'm going to camp somewhere under this pass. You do what you want to do."

"We could—"

Slocum extended his hand toward the trail off the mountain. "Have at her."

Combs made a displeased face and shook his head. Slocum knew he had won that argument. "Let's make camp then," he said and led the roan from the pass.

• • •

Dawn came like a cold blanket. Gray clouds were gathering. They fled out of the northwest and promised moisture. Slocum collected the horses with an eye to the sky. He led them back to camp as Combs built up the fire.

Slocum began to saddle the three. Combs boiled water for coffee and soon fried some fatback in a skillet. The saddling completed, Slocum took his jumper from the bedroll and buttoned it up against the sharp wind.

"May snow," Combs said when he joined him.

"It could this high up. I've seen it snow in August before in the high country like this." Slocum squatted on his boot heels to let the heat from the fire radiate off his face and warmed his outstretched hands.

"You have any idea where this buck's headed?"

"Some sacred place for a medicine man, I reckon."

"Hogwash. That's all bullshit, you know it. He's going up there and assault my wife."

"I only saw the man once. He was out to steal that roan horse and I missed hitting him."

"Damn shame you missed him. What happened to Ruff?"

"The cowboy with the mustache?"

"Yeah, you didn't know him?"

"No, I found him dead in the chicken yard. Three bullet holes in his chest. I buried him."

Combs nodded he heard him and used a kerchief for a hot holder to pour coffee in his tin cup. "Them red bastards all need to be shipped out of here."

"This was their land," Slocum said and blew the steam away.

"Hell, they won't do nothing with it but plant a damn tepee and shit outside the door. There's lots of good timber and grazing up there on what they gave them lazy red devils."

"Guess you're entitled to your opinion."

"Well, gawdamnit, a minute ago you said you shot at him."

"I shot at him because he was trying to steal my horse. I'd shoot at you if you tried the same thing. Not 'cause he was an Apache."

Combs rose and glared out at the mountains beyond. "They need exterminated or all moved to the Indian Nation."

"Maybe that's what has them all on the warpath."

"No. They're bloodthirsty savages and ain't no cuddling or hellfire and brimstone missionaries going to change them either."

Combs fished some of the crisp back fat out and, along with Mrs. Tatum's cold biscuits, served them to Slocum on his tin plate.

"Thanks," Slocum said, rose and went off to eat in peace.

Why did this man irritate him so? He hoped before sundown they found and recovered his wife. The sooner he and Combs parted company the better it would be. The food eaten, they drank the last cup of coffee at the dying fire. The temperature had not risen and the fresh wind swept Slocum's whiskers as he finished the final sip with the grounds.

Both men mounted up and Slocum took the lead down the trail. Grateful to at last be under the mountain, the roan had proven himself surefooted. The only thing that upset Slocum was the fact that they were in the open for Red Elk to pick them off if he had a high-powered rifle. The barren, steep face of the mountain side offered no cover above or beneath them.

From his vantage point Slocum could see across the deep chasm and watched a herd of elk big as ants grazing in the park country. He pointed them out to Combs, who nodded that he had seen them.

"One of them would sure beat fatback," Combs said.

Slocum agreed with a nod about the elk meat, but he didn't want a rifle shot to warn the Apache they were coming. For the next while they would need to be satisfied with fatback. At least it didn't have maggots in it like that served during the war that they were forced to eat or starve.

The creak of the saddle leather, the ring of iron shoes on rock outcroppings accompanied them. In places, the roan's footing even slipped, but he quickly regained it, gathering up under him. The prints of the dun's iron shoes were still evident where they passed through ahead of him and Combs.

At noontime, they reached the valley floor with a small, silver stream. After a quick check, Slocum decided that Red Elk and her had watered their animal here. He studied the prints carefully and looked off to the west where they had headed.

"They camp here?" Combs asked.

Slocum shook his head. "Only watered their horses."

"What's the plan?"

"Let the horses graze here for a while. This looks like good grass. Wasn't much up there and they need to eat, can't tell where we'll be at dark."

"Graze?"

"Yes, you didn't bring enough grain to feed them."

"How damn far ahead are they?"

"Maybe a day's ride or less." Slocum loosened the cinch on the roan.

"This is a waste—"

"Listen, Combs, you got a better plan, head your ass up that trail. I'm letting my horse graze some. They ain't going far on an empty belly."

"But when we catch them—"

"If I thought they were that close I'd push on. We need these horses too bad to push them past the point of their endurance."

Combs scowled and dropped out of the saddle. "What you're doing now?"

"Going to cut me a willow and see if I can catch some trout to supplement your back fat."

"There any in there?" Combs asked, peering in the crystal-clear water.

"I hope so," Slocum said and stuck his hunting knife in the soft earth. Then, with a small stone, he began to hit the handle.

"What the hell is that for?"

"Calling up worms."

Combs snorted, then he stopped to stare when a wriggling earthworm came out on the surface. "By gawd, you did it."

With the catgut line on the end of his pole, Slocum cast the fat, red worm into the swirling eddy formed by some large rocks. The pole bobbed over hard and he swung a silver cutthroat out on the bank. It danced and flopped in the grass as he went to unhook it.

"Better cut a willow stick for a stringer," he said to the frowning Combs. "He's supper and we need three more."

Chapter 9

The rain held off until late afternoon. The daylight grew dimmer, and then it began as ice pellets. Slocum shook out his slicker. Small diamonds danced off the canvas cloth and his hat brim as he pushed the roan northward.

"We get much rain we'll lose their tracks," Combs complained. "Taking that much time was a waste."

Slocum waved his hand at the man to signal he heard him. There was no reasoning with Combs when he had a mindset. Still, the meal of fresh trout had warmed him a lot, plus the roan had his fill of good grass and so did the other two animals. There were no livery stables out there to furnish them remounts. They were miles from anywhere; in fact, the closest might be southern Colorado, over a hundred miles north.

They pushed until dark and made camp along a steam. Slocum unsaddled the animals and hobbled them. They would need a lean-to, he searched around while Combs worked on starting a fire. The cold rain fell like a mist. But everything was wet including Slocum's boots.

He took the camp ax and went up in the timber to fell some poles for the shelter. The wet boughs rained more on him as he felled them and then stripped off the branches. With a small pine tree on one side, he lashed together a tepee pole setup to hold up the other side of the front rail. That complete, he began to chop out the roof sticks; ordinarily he would use boughs for the roof, but they would not deflect the rain. He intended to use the pack tarp to stretch over it to shed the moisture.

Combs grumbled out loud about the wet wood fire not starting, while Slocum completed the shelter. At last, he noticed the flames began to lick the steady, fine downpour. Their gear stored inside, he came over, squatted down and poured himself some coffee.

"It ain't the Grand Hotel, but it'll beat getting wet all night."

Combs cast a critical look at the shelter in the fire's orange light. "Yeah, guess it'll work."

Slocum didn't bother to comment. It would damn sure beat sitting up all night in his slicker. Lots of times he had been forced to do just that during the war and even after that with bounty hunters on his tracks.

"How long is this going take," Combs asked, "to catch up with them?"

Slocum looked in his tin cup, then raised his gaze. "I don't know, but for her safety I don't want to go off half-cocked."

"Her safety?" Combs scoffed at him. "Why, that red bastard has been screwing her ass off the whole time."

"Think what you want. I'm not risking her life by going in there half-cocked."

"Half-cocked, hell, we haven't even found them."

"I've tracked down wolves in winter. You get on their trail and dog them. Pretty soon they get curious and raise up and look back. You don't look at them, keep walking up their tracks, soon they're whining and more curious."

"You think we'll do that to Red Elk?"

Slocum nodded as a thin stream of water ran off his hat brim. "I aim to walk him down."

"You don't understand—he has my wife up there."

"Combs, I didn't join up with you because I particularly like your company. I too am concerned about your wife. You know I met her and brought her to Tatum's outpost?"

"Did she say anything about me?"

Slocum shook his head. "She was under lots of stress from the attack."

"You think she's crazy?"

"I think that she's been through a helluva lot. That would drive anyone off their normal way of life."

"There wasn't a damn thing wrong with her when I left." Combs forked out some back fat and put a couple more biscuits on his plate.

"I'm going to the shelter," Slocum announced and took his plate and cup there.

"How bad was she?" Comb asked, joining him.

"Bad? I wouldn't say bad. Mixed up perhaps, confused, but not bad."

They both grew silent as the rain drummed on the tarp.

Thunder awoke Slocum in the night. He slept in his wet boots satisfied he would never get them on again if he removed them. Concerned, he put on his slicker and went to check on the horses. The bolts of dancing lightning gave him windows of opportunity to make out the horses standing hipshot. He vented his bladder and then went back.

"Everything all right?" Combs grunted at him.

"Yeah, fine." Back under the covers, he listened to the *tap-tap* of the rain on the tarp. More thunder rolled across the mountains and whitened the night in blinding flashes.

Wet to the skin, that was how he recalled the sloppy roads with ruts knee-deep in Virginia. The dogwoods were blooming, the only bright thing that wasn't wrinkled like a prune from all the rain. A soldier had no thoughts but the drudgery of putting one foot down and another after it, hoping the roads didn't suck off his worn-out shoes. Nothing dry, and no rations for two days.

Then an officer on horseback rode up and told him to take six men and forage the area for food. He looked around at the rock-and-split log fences. The old, weathered, broke-down cornstalks beyond that wouldn't even make good feed for a horse. Find food was what the man meant.

He chose the best men in his company and agreed to rejoin the company at the next crossroads—a place called Congress Church. They struck out wearing their canvas ponchos soaked through, the wax dressing worn out by the elements.

They found burned-out farmhouses. Empty outbuildings, not a chicken or hog left on the place though the aroma of their excrement still hung in the air. The men crowded inside the empty fowl coop, grateful for the moment's respite to be out of the beating rain that drummed on the roof and the roll of thunder like a carpet spread over the wide valley.

He sent Corporal Thymes and three men to the east with orders, regardless of what they found, to return there before dark to meet him and his two men. Corporal Thymes gone with his three into the gray half-light of drizzle, he led his two soldiers through fields and woods in an easterly direction.

The smell of wood smoke reached his nostrils and he raised his hand to halt his men. He tried to pick it up again. Where there was smoke, there was fire and humans. They might or might not have food. They could be enemy or deserters. Deserters were worse than enemies. Yankees expected to be taken prisoner; deserters feared the firing squad, so they seldom surrendered.

He and his men worked their way uphill through the wet trees. The heavy drops of rain slapped their heads as the branches collected water and released it in big gobs. Then they could hear voices. Slocum signaled for them to halt. He could see these men had hung a hog. It had been scraped and gutted.

He moved back and told both men to load their rifles. There would be a chance that they wouldn't even fire.

"How many?" Irwin asked under his breath.

"Three or four."

"Who are they?"

"Deserters or bushwhackers."

The men nodded that they understood and loaded their rifles.

"They don't obey my order, you shoot to kill."

"We will, Sarge."

Slocum hoped the revolver in his waistband would fire. They advanced on the party.

"Hands in the air!" Slocum shouted. Thunder echoed his words and the men jumped for their weapons. Both of the rifles answered and cut down a man apiece. Slocum's own pistol misfired the first cylinder, then he snapped off a shot that cut down the third man.

"I surrender! I surrender!"

"You reb or Yankee?" Irwin asked with his reloaded rifle pointed at the man.

"Reb!" The man's words were too late; Irwin's rifle blasted an orange flame out of the muzzle and the bullet struck the man in the face.

"Lying sumbitch," Irwin swore.

The weapons of the dead men were gathered, then the three examined the half-grown pig's carcass.

"Like Christmas," Irwin said. "We ought to cut us a hunk off and roast it right here."

"No. We must share it with the company."

Irwin wiped at his mouth corners for the drool. "Where you reckon they found that rascal at?"

"One that got away."

"Load the bastard up. The sooner we share him, the better my belly will feel."

"Why, he won't give more'n a bite apiece to our outfit," Irwin said, shouldering the pig as Slocum let it down by the rope.

"One more bite than we had," Slocum said and looked over the four prone men. He wasn't sure they were all dead but they would be. He carried Irwin's rifle and led the way off the mountain in the drizzling rain and under the thunder.

Good thing they found the hog because that was all his outfit had to eat for two more days. Under the pattern of the rain on the tarp, Slocum laid there and tried to recall how good the pork had tasted, but he couldn't draw up any recollection. It must have been a treat, he decided.

At dawn, the downpour let up, but the thick clouds overhead persisted. They ate cold biscuits, swept down with reheated coffee, saddled their animals, loaded the packs on and headed north up the trail.

"We've lost the trail," Combs complained as they forded the rushing stream now knee-deep on their horses.

"I'm not certain," Slocum said and pushed the roan up the slick bank. For certain the prints were not there to follow and he must use his instinct and hope to find some sign. They moved northward without more than a few scattered tracks barely legible to try and decipher as Red Elk's.

Close to noon, Slocum thought he heard something and

motioned for them to take to the timber close by. Back in the grove of quaking aspen, he used his scope. Across the valley he spotted several painted horses. Through the glass he studied the boys driving them. They must be near a large Apache camp.

"What is it?"

"Not good news. I think that Red Elk may have gone back to a village."

"I thought that he—"

Slocum shook his head. "Hell, all I know is what them young boys said. That he was headed for some sacred place."

"What're we going to do now?"

"Scout some and see if we can locate her. It might be possible to sneak her away from them."

"Hellfire, if we'd overtook them like I wanted to do—"

"Shut up, Combs. We didn't and now we must see if he stopped over here."

"Well, didn't I—"

"Shut up, I've had belly of your good ideas. You got one now?" He frowned at the man seated on his horse.

"No."

"Till you do, quit your bitching." Slocum looked again through the glass. How big was their camp and how far away was it? Their horse herd might be the answer. Drive it off and distract the warriors. He wished he had only himself to think about; besides the know-it-all, Combs had proved to be a carper as well.

Chapter 10

"You see anyone looks like her?" Combs whispered.

Slocum swung the telescope's lens across the camp. No sign of a white woman or his dun horse, the two things he felt would mark Red Elk's presence. There were some two dozen tepees and lots of squaws and children running about. Food looked like the thing they lacked. He saw no deer or elk being butchered. In a camp of that size several such animals were needed for consumption each day.

Some of the women had returned with baskets full of berries, but fruit would hardly sustain life. Obviously, most of the men were not present or they would be sitting in a circle smoking and telling great tales in the middle of the camp. So the men might be either on the warpath or hunting. It would be the time to charge in and rescue Dorothy with the least resistance and greatest chance for success.

"They down there?" Combs grumbled with impatience in his tone.

"They may be inside a tepee or simply out of sight."

"Yeah. Probably screwing their ass off—"

Slocum looked over and frowned at the man. Then he turned back; Combs grew worse with each passing day. Recovering a hostage was no hit and run ordeal, it required plenty of patience. One needed to be certain they could get her out alive or not try. In the last minutes, many times, captives were slain. That was why they couldn't take any chances.

"If he ain't here—what then?"

"We need to find him."

"Hell, that could take forever."

"You can clear out."

"No, gawdamn her, I want her found!"

Slocum studied the man and then shook his head in disbelief before he turned back to look through the scope. After a couple of hours, they pulled back from their place in the timber overlooking the Apaches to their dry camp. Eating jerky, they huddled under blankets. The weather had not warmed much.

"How we going to find out where this Red Elk is at?"

"Perhaps capture a berry picker and get out of her where he went."

"A berry picker?" Combs frowned.

"Yes, several woman have being leaving camp to go and pick berries today. We might single out one of them and quiz her."

"Ain't that dangerous?"

"Hell, being here is dangerous. I've found Indian woman more receptive than their men to conversation."

"You got some charm you work on them?"

"Yeah, it's only obvious to squaws."

"Whores, ain't they?"

"Not the ones I knew, but I guess there are some."

"Diseased whores. They all have the clap."

"Probably got it from a white man too," Slocum said and lay down to go to sleep.

"You going to bed?"

"Yeah, you're sitting up for guard, it don't take two." Slocum nestled his head on the blanket.

"What about tonight?"

"Apaches hate the night. They won't kill you at night."

"How come?"

"Superstitious as hell."

Combs snorted through his nose. "I don't believe that."

"Then you sit up all night." Slocum closed his eyes.

• • •

He awoke from his sleep. Wary of the reason for his being awake, he studied the stars and felt for the Colt out of habit. With an ear turned, he listened carefully to sort out any strange sounds. The soft grunts of his sleeping animals and the shuffle of their feet close by. He rose in a crouch. They were in the thick pine bough cover. He walked to the edge of the bluff they were camped upon. In the pearly light, he tried to see anything unusual on the move beneath his perch. Far to the east the great pony herd was being held, but it was too far to distinguish.

Then he stepped back and drained his bladder. In the morning he needed to apprehend a berry picker, preferably a young girl who might be bribed into telling them the whereabouts of Red Elk. Perhaps he could talk Combs into staying behind, as two of them would be easier to spot than one. Besides, he might make some sense with her and all Combs would do is rant anyway. Finished pissing, he put it away.

Strange how the man talked about his wife. Like he didn't want her back—but still he came and invested in the search. Had he done that for show, so he could tell her daddy all he did to try and find her? Slocum shook his head before he climbed back under the cover in the predawn coolness. No telling about Combs.

"Go by yourself—"

"Yes, you keep the pack horse. I ain't back by night, then you head for home."

"That mean the Injuns will have got you?"

"They might. I can't capture a berry picker and get back, then you vamoose."

"Why—"

"Listen, I've explained it twice. They won't see one as easy as two. I get in there, get her and get back."

"What if they track you back here?"

"Then we've both got troubles."

Combs shook his head. "All right, then you go and I'll stay here. But come dark I'm leaving, you're here or not."

"Fine."

"Your neck."

"My neck."

"What if he ain't been here or you don't learn anything? What then?"

"We go to Plan B."

"What in hell's Plan B?"

"I ain't got it figured out yet. Maybe you can while I'm gone today."

"Bullshit."

"Yeah, there's a lot of that." Slocum took his saddle and pad and tossed it on the roan. He jerked up the girth. He'd spent some long days in the saddle looking for a Comanche captive. This one would be no different. It sure wasn't like a cattle-buying trip; Combs would learn patience or turn back.

He swung up on the roan and looked at the man. "By dark." Then with a hand salute, he rode off up into the timber. He needed to find a course to circle back off the mountainside undetected and find the berry patches in the bottoms. The sun coming up in the east, he worked his way westward on the game trails.

In the middle of the morning, he spooked a good-size cinnamon bear. The bruin raised up, gave a snort and rushed away down hill. No sign of a cub, the bear looked young and probably a male, though sexing bears on the run was not easy.

When Slocum decided he was far enough west, he came down through a ravine of quaking aspens. He left the roan in the tree cover and worked his way to the edge for better view of the bottoms.

He spotted a lone picker. Over the rush of the small creek he could hear the bells on her basket making a clicking sound to scare off any near by bears. Then further up he noticed a sow with two cubs cross the creek and start toward the woman. No way that woman picking could know about the danger. Sows with cubs were deadly business in a berry patch or any place if she considered them in danger; the sow would fight a buzz saw. Certainly the female would attack any human she thought might harm them.

Slocum hurried back to his roan. He swung up and jerked the Winchester out of the scabbard. Even if his actions scared the woman away, he needed to make sure she didn't get mauled by the sow. With a short "he-yah," he sent the roan down the hill.

The woman's dark eyes looked startled at him as the powerful horse plunged downhill in the loose rock. Slocum pointed his rifle to the west to emphasize the bear's presence. She turned, looked, dropped her basket and began to run.

The wrong thing. The female, seeing the movement, came bounding through the brambles. The roan hit the creek and he slapped him hard to make him splash across the creek and gain the far bank. They were ahead of the grizzly, but not all the lead that Slocum wanted. He could see the fleeing woman leaping through the briars, mouth open as he sent the roan after her. The bear wasn't making a hard charge or he would have had to consider shooting her. Still, he could hear her loud woofs and the crash of brambles behind him as he bore down on the girl with her whirling buckskin fringe.

He switched hands with the rifle bend low and swept her up. Then holding her across his lap, guiding the roan with his gun hand, he booted another burst of speed out of the gelding. They flew through the creek and up the gravelly bank. He slid the pony to a stop, satisfied Mrs. Bear no longer wanted them.

The short Indian woman looked into his eyes and shook her head as if she could not believe who he was.

Slocum reached back and shoved the rifle in the scabbard, then righted himself.

"Buenos dias," he said to her.

"Who are you?" she asked in Spanish, shaking her head in dismay.

He guessed her to be in her late teens. Short, but her firm breasts pushed out the beaded blouse, and she had a slender nose for an Indian and a full bottom lip. Her hair hung in fur-wrapped braids, her legs encased in deerskin and her moccasins were decorated in colorful beads too.

"Slocum."

"Two Bird."

He nodded and the roan began to walk. He made no move to stop him.

"You saved my life. Why?" She frowned distrustfully at him.

"Need your help. I am looking for Red Elk."

"Why?"

"He has a man's woman."

She nodded. "The woman is in the spirit world."

"The man wants his wife back."

"Red Elk is in the mountains. He thinks this woman has answers for our tribe."

Slocum shook his head. "She's in white spirits."

Two Bird used the horn and scooted around to make herself more comfortable. "Where will you take me?"

"I would let you go."

"I owe you," she said and did not move.

"Married?"

She shook her braids. Slocum knew she had been married, too old not to have been, but Apaches never spoke of the dead; it was bad luck. She was not married at the present time; there are ways women act with men after they lose their innocence. Still, she was attractive and smelled of wild berries. A sweet perfume that ran up his nose. Her small fingers that clutched the cap of his saddle horn were even black stained.

"Why do you want her?"

"I only want the woman back for her husband."

She chewed on her full bottom lip as if considering him.

"I would be dead if the she bear had caught me. I will take you there."

Slocum looked back up the bottom. The huge grizzly sow raised up and turned her head inspectively at him even at the distance. He nodded he had heard Two Bird's decision and set the roan up the mountain. They would need to make tracks out of there—the roan's prints all over the bottoms would sure alert the camp when they came to pick or to look for her.

They reached Combs and the camp by noontime. The man rose, squinted and shook his head in disapproval at the sight of her.

"He ain't Señor Nice," Slocum warned her in Spanish before they reached the man.

She nodded she heard him.

"Two Bird meet Milton Combs," he said, dismounting and then taking her off by the waist. She wasn't bigger than nothing. On the ground beside him, she didn't measure four feet tall.

"She's a woman?" Combs asked with a frown of disbelief.

"Yes. I saved her from a grizzly this morning. She's taking us to Red Elk's camp."

Combs tossed his head in her direction, then whispered, "You trust her."

"Yeah, you don't?"

"No. Why, she's liable to slip a frog sticker in you while you sleep."

"Combs, she's all we have. I got real lucky getting her away from that grizzly. Now you act friendly, 'cause we don't know where Red Elk is and she does."

The man frowned at him. "She know about my wife?"

"Yes, she does."

"She's—my wife, Dorothy, is she all right?" he asked Slocum again. "She was alive?"

"Yes, load up," Slocum ordered. "I left too many tracks to stay here long."

"Guess so. What's she going to ride?"

"The roan double with me."

Slocum picked up the pack saddle and began to rig the bay. Unasked, Two Bird went on the far side and helped straighten things. When Slocum loaded the first pannier he gave her a wink and a grin in gratitude. She nodded and quickly shifted the horse around by the lead so he didn't have to go around to hang the other pannier. The second one in place, he tossed on the tarp and she helped make the diamond hitch.

Combs was sitting on his horse. Slocum ignored him and swung aboard the roan, then lowered his arm and swiftly swung her on behind him.

"Which way?" he asked her over his shoulder.

She pointed uphill. He rode past Combs, who muttered, "I damn sure hope this ain't some kind of a trap she's taking us to."

"Have the faith," Slocum said as she took a hold around his waist and forced her rock-hard breasts in his back. He damn sure had better company. Now all she had to do was lead them to Red Elk's camp. Then he realized she might not have had much to eat of late. He found some jerky in his vest pocket and offered it to her as they went up the game trail through the timber.

She never hesitated taking the dried meat and soon chomped on it. *Forty miles of hell.* Slocum considered, then perhaps they would find poor Dorothy. He looked back and saw Combs bringing on the pack horse. The sour look on his face would have clabbered a vat of fresh milk. Then Slocum chuckled to himself, strongly aware of her presence behind him and enjoying the company. Blasting sticks came in small packages too. He glanced up the steep game trail ahead of them. *We're coming, Dorothy, quick as we can.*

Chapter 11

They worked their way the rest of the day toward a saddle in the range she indicated they must cross through. Slocum felt good. Her knowledge of the country was worth a fortune they'd lost in wasted time of the two white men trying to find Red Elk's trail. Slocum paused to rest their horses on a great bench carpeted in grass and let the horses graze, while Combs looked sour-faced over the delay but remained tight-lipped. For Slocum's money, the man should have realized the need for their animals' nutrition or they'd be on foot trekking for civilization without his wife.

Two Bird brought Slocum his tin cup full of spring water. He scoped the mountainside ahead and found nothing, save some real elk. No way to know how far away Red Elk's camp was, so he dared not shoot any game for fear the rifle report would put the medicine man on his guard.

"She say how far away it is?" Combs asked.

"Two Bird?" Slocum called to her in Spanish. "How far?"

"Two days." Then she shrugged and made the hand sign they must go over the mountain and then to the left.

'What the hell does two days mean?" Combs stood directly in front of him.

"Two dawns and two sunsets."

"Damnit to hell, Slocum, does that mean walking or running or trotting?"

"Indians are vague about distance. They've got a place on

the western side of the Bighorns called Ten Sleep. Meant you was halfway from Fort Laramie to Yellowstone, but it didn't say walk, run or fly to make it there in ten days."

Combs shook his head, took off his hat and ran his fingers through his hair. "I think all this is waste of good time. That damn Apache's probably tired of screwing her and hit her in the head by this time."

"Free country. You can turn around and go back."

"You mean you would ride on without supplies and look for her?"

"You heard me, Combs. You can hear."

"You know what Tatum said, she was crazy. She's probably worse nuts now."

Slocum drove his fist in Combs's gut. It drove the air from him for a minute. Ready for whatever Combs wanted to do about it, Slocum waited. The man's eyes wide open, he glared at Slocum. Then, as if he had reconsidered doing anything, he went away in a huff.

"What . . . the hell you do . . . that for?" Combs asked over his shoulder.

"Teach you a lesson, Combs. You went off and left her. Far as I'm concerned when you rode off, you left her. All you can say is bad things about a poor woman been through fourteen kinds of hell, then keep you mouth shut." Slocum started to turn away.

"You got a thing going with my wife?"

He whirled back and pointed a finger like a gun at the man. "You don't go to speaking better of her, I'll make a thing out of you."

"I ain't scared of you, Slocum."

"Mind what I said."

"She's my wife and I can do whatever I want to her and say whatever I want about her. You can't stop me."

Slocum nodded his head with a shortness. He wet his lower lip, still gazing at the man's back. "You lay a hand on her, I'll break it so you can't ever use it."

"We ain't talking about no Indian whore here. She's my wife, not yours."

"Combs, you heard what I said. Won't be no court of law protect you either."

"Maybe you raped my wife and that's why she ran away with the gawdamn Indians."

Slocum looked him up and down. The rage felt like a great ball in his chest. Damn, if he'd been Dorothy, he'd have left with Ruff too. Then he turned to the short Indian woman. "Gather the horse, we're parting company."

"All right—all right—maybe—maybe, I've been upset and said something I didn't mean. We've come this far together. It can't be—let's say, two more days to get to his camp, I'll not say another word about my wife, you or her." He motioned to Two Bird.

"Fine, remember that." Slocum went off after her.

"He is angry inside," she said under her breath when Slocum joined her.

"He better learn I ain't putting up with him or his mouth."

She gave him a private smile, then fended ducking her head. "I thought you would kill him."

"He wasn't worth it." Slocum vaulted in the saddle and then bent over to hoist her up behind him.

They set out up the trail that led west. The sun was already behind the mountain range towering over them. In less than an hour they would need to make camp for the night. Had they come one day or were there two days left, he wondered as they rode on.

The sway of the horse's gait was under him, the small woman sat at his back, the cooler temperatures were settling in and wind was sweeping his face. They still had miles to cross, no matter the time.

Combs said little over the meal. Finished, he took his bedroll several feet from the small fire that Slocum risked because the wind was westerly and swept the smoke toward their back trail. Besides, they needed a real meal and both men ate with relish the beans and rice seasoned with a can of tomatoes and some chilies. It beat the jerky, crackers and dry cheese flavor. Slocum noticed she finished her plate, eating after the men in squaw fashion. He never bothered to try and change her habit.

The man covered his head with his blanket as if to hide and Slocum dismissed him. When Two Bird finished washing the plates and utensils, she joined Slocum for a cup of coffee sweetened with brown sugar. The flavor drew a smile on her face.

"No woman?" she asked, meaning, did he have one?

Slocum shook his head. "No man?"

She dropped her gaze and gave him a like sign. Apaches never spoke the name of their dead. So if her husband were dead, she would not say his name nor much more than he already knew about the matter.

"No food in camp?" he asked.

"Little," she said. "The men are at war. Agent say, we can't go hunt the buffalo. What could they do?"

"Buffalo are gone."

Her eyes widened and she shook her head. "I have seen them. They were like flocks of many birds. Too many to count out there." She indicated the east and meant on the far plains of the Illano Estacato.

"They killed them."

"But they must have killed so many—"

"White hunters with great guns."

"Oh, no. My people will starve. The deer, the elk are too shy from loud bullets to ever kill with an arrow."

"I heard your people had new rifles."

"The agent will take them away. He did before."

"When you came into the agency, starving, for food?"

She nodded.

Slocum sipped on the rich coffee. Somewhere higher on the mountain, a wolf howled at the rising moon. She rose and came to sit beside him as if he would protect her. He tossed out the coarse grounds and another lobo answered. Wolves and white men were a lot alike. They were the high end of the predators. All others were subjected to their rules. Tonight a mule deer or elk would learn of their sharp teeth. Down the mountain, in the Apache camp, the fangs of hunger would pain the families of the warriors.

"You want more food?" he asked.

She shook her head.

"Been a long day. Do you wish to sleep alone?"

Then another wolf called out and her fingers sought his arm. She spoke in Spanish. "I will sleep in your blankets."

"Fine, roll them out," he said and went to check on the horses. He could make out their outlines in the starlit

meadow. After checking the hobbles on each he finished with
the roan and slapped him fondly on the neck. Good thing
that Red Elk didn't know that the big gelding was this close
or he'd be there after him.

He drained his bladder in the last slit of pearly light that
bathed the mountain pass, thought for a moment about the
small Apache woman and headed that way. He laid his holster beside the bedroll where it would be handy and sat down
to remove his boots. She was already in the covers. He
stripped off his vest, shirt and pants, slipping under his so-
gans and canvas cover in his underwear.

He rolled over to face her and she ran a hand over the
whiskers on his face. Made him wish he had shaved. Too
late for that. Then his hand discovered that she was naked
and her smooth skin glided under his hand. She moved
closer. When his hand cupped her small teardrop breast she
let out a sharp exhale and inched against him.

He carefully tested it until the nipple hardened like a rock.
Her breathing quickened and she sent his hand lower on her
stomach. With her legs spread apart she inserted his finger
inside her. Then her eyes closed in pleasure and she raised
her butt off the blanket to meet his thrusts. Her small finger
soon caught the head of his hardened dick and she pulled
him on top of her, all the time increasing the flow to stiffen
it more with her pumping hand.

Soon he braced himself above her and was pounding himself into her palace of pleasure. The walls grew tighter
around his sword and she arched her back. The hot rush of
her come swept by his probe. But she never quit, and filled
with the urge for more and more, she pulled him deeper
inside her until their pelvic bones were hard pressed against
each other on the downstroke. Then, with both of them wild
with the fires of their passion, he stove it all the way in and
exploded inside her. They wilted in an exhausted pile. He
eased himself off of her, dazzled, still dizzy and spent.

She rose on her arm and ran a hand down the side of his
face. "I will be here for you."

He nodded he heard her. Then she nestled against his side.
He looked at the stars and the constellations. By dawn, they
needed to be in the saddle and on their way. Maybe Combs
had learned his lesson. But Slocum feared it was only a short

truce until the man could find a place to take his advantage. He better start sleeping with one eye open. With a great yawn that closed his eyes and made the water spurt from them, he waited until they refocused on the stars. Combs would bear watching from there on.

Dorothy, we are coming for you.

Chapter 12

They crossed over the pass above the timberline in the cold
predawn. Far off in the land of the Taos' gods, the sun
peeked from under a dark blue, felt blanket. Slocum led the
way. The ring of their horses' shoes clanged on the gray
rocks that looked freshly broken apart. Their edges were like
knives and it would be easy to quicken a pony in such footing. He didn't hurry over them, but let the roan pick his way.
Slocum wondered when Combs would bitch about their lack
of speed, but the man only swore at his horse and the reluc-
tant pack animal.

The basin below, still shrouded in night, looked gray and
gloomy beneath them. Slocum was anxious to be in the timber cover and not exposed for Red Elk's or any other brown
eyes to spot. The roan went stiff legged off the sharp trail
and for the first time, Slocum felt easier at his discovery.
Another iron-shod horse had been on this trail a few days
before. Was it his dun or another horse stolen from white
men? He couldn't be certain, but it raised the odds that Two
Bird knew of this place and was sending them there. While
he had no doubts that she was honest, he held some doubts
that she could actually go to such a sacred place that few
women ever saw, save the few female warriors that were rare
or a woman out of her head like Dorothy. "Possessed" would
be the better word.

The medicine man sought to speak to the hereafter through

Dorothy and his whole hopes were that this woman could see them or had been there herself. Who knew? Perhaps Dorothy had been there. She didn't act right, didn't know him from Ruff. Tough thing, some women returned from such hells and made a life for themselves, others that he knew never came back.

He twisted in the saddle and saw Combs was coming. Good enough. From behind him on the saddle, Two Bird took a better hold of him. Wrapped in one of his blankets against the morning chill, she drew herself to him and rested her head on his back.

"Long ways to fall." She meant the looming thousands of feet to the left side of the trail.

"Better sprout wings, you go off there."

"*Si,*" she agreed.

The trail down the yellow-faced mountain looked more like a wrinkle than a pathway. All Slocum could think about was reaching the timberline and cover. At last in the stunted pines, he dismounted on a flat ledge big enough to accommodate their animals. Despite the morning cold, Combs mopped his sweaty face with a kerchief.

"Damned tough ride off of there," he said, looking close to exhaustion.

"It should get better. We've got some trees for cover from here on."

"Man went off up there, he'd fall for two days."

Slocum agreed.

"Guess I lost it yesterday. Sorry about that. I ought to be grateful you're doing this, I damn sure couldn't find her by myself."

"No apology necessary. These animals are getting done in. We get off this mountain we may have to rest them for a while."

Combs nodded in agreement and remopped his face. The high altitude obviously was wearing on the man. Slocum felt the small rap of a headache himself that he usually experienced the first days in the high country, but it wasn't serious.

"You going to be all right to go on?" Slocum asked him.

"Yeah, sure, I'm fine."

"Good," Slocum said, but not certain the man was telling him everything.

"We go now?" she asked, jumping to her feet.

He nodded and climbed on the roan, then pulled her up. Combs mounted with some effort and waved him on. Satisfied the man was in the saddle and coming, Slocum booted the roan off the mountain through the stunted pines. Gnarled and twisted by centuries of wind and powerful storms, they hardly looked like they belonged to the same species as those lower down that reached to the sky in unbent lines.

By late afternoon, they arrived in a wide valley bisected by a clear stream. Slocum nodded to all the grass and she slid to the ground.

"How far away is Red Elk?" he asked, dropping heavily to the ground and letting his sea legs stiffen to support him.

"In that canyon." She pointed. Slocum guessed the distance in the long shadows for the cut in the range to be ten miles away. The clear air was deceiving and he hoped it was that close.

"Does he have a cave or a camp?"

"Camp."

Slocum nodded. He undid the cinch straps with stiff fingers and tried to test the wind. If there were cutthroats in the stream, they would need to make a small fire to cook them. He glanced over and saw Combs was seated on a log and looked winded.

"I'm fine." He waved away Slocum's hard look.

"Go unpack the horse," he said under his breath to her.

She hurried over and brought the bay to where his saddle was upended. In a flash, the diamond hitch was undone and tarp taken off. Slocum took down the first pannier and started taking the second one off, seeing Combs still sat on the log.

He swung it to the ground, then he went over to where the man sat.

"You all right?"

"I will be in a minute. Got a little light-headed when I dismounted. I'll be fine." Combs rubbed his palms on his pants' legs. "Never had the high country bother me like this before."

"You sit. We'll catch a few fish. You want a drink?"

"Yeah, I got some whiskey in my saddlebags."

Slocum meant water, but he found the bottle and gave it

to the man. Combs uncorked the bottle and took a few deep snorts. "Here, it's good whiskey."

"I didn't doubt it. I'll hobble your horse for you." He dismissed the man's offer to help him.

"I can—" The man sat back down.

"You better stay hooked." Slocum finished fitting the sorrel with his restrains and swept off the bridle. "Anything I can get you?"

Combs shook his head wearily and waved him away with the whiskey bottle. "I'll be fine. Just feeling a little under the weather is all."

Two Bird followed Slocum to the stream. He found a green sapling for a pole, attached the line, them drummed up some dark worms. On his hook, he sent the segmented critter into the swirling water that swept it into a larger eddy. The pole dipped, he set back on it and out of the surface came a ten-inch sliver cutthroat, dancing on his tail. Two Bird rushed down to the edge to take it off the hook.

"You eat fish?" Slocum asked her in Spanish.

She turned with the ten-inch fish strung through the gill on her fingers and nodded.

"Good," he said and strung another worm on the rig. Most Apaches did not eat them. Part of their superstition that made the trout fishing so good in the lands they claimed.

The next three he hooked and delivered were in the eight-inch class, but it was enough for a meal. Combs was in his bedroll when they returned. Slocum went by to check on him and asked with concern about his condition.

"I'll sleep it off," the man said and turned back to go to sleep.

"We have some fresh fish?"

Combs shook his head.

"What is wrong?" she asked in Spanish, when Slocum returned to where she built a pit fire. Apaches had skill at making smokeless fires in holes they dug in the ground with knives. Obviously she was making such a setup to cook their fish.

"He's sick. Won't say much. Wants to sleep."

She nodded she heard him, then shook her head as if she didn't know what to do either.

He glanced back toward the man. Combs' ailment better

not be too serious; there wasn't a doctor in four days of this place. If he grew worse and couldn't ride then they would need to take him out by travois. Crossing those passes they came in over would be sheer hell and dangerous too. Slocum shook his head to try and clear out his dread of the possibilities. Then he dismissed it; the things that one worried the most about never happened.

Full of the fresh, mild-tasting fish she cooked, they sat and listened to the night birds with blankets over their shoulders against the cool air coming in on a soft wind.

"Red Elk's place is that close. I'll ride up there and scout it out tomorrow. You better stay here and watch him."

She agreed with a nod.

"We can get Dorothy away from him, we can start back."

"What if he has killed her?"

"Same thing, we go back."

"What about him?" She tossed her head toward Combs.

"We better hope he feels better in the morning."

"Where will you go?"

"When this is over?"

"*Si.*"

He looked up at the star-studded sky. "I'm not certain. You know a place where we can kill an elk for meat and be unbothered?"

"Oh, *si.*"

"We might go there afterward."

She hugged his arm and pressed her face to it.

"Not forever," he said to her. Then he thought about the Abbott Brothers, Lyle and Ferd, the Fort Scott, Kansas, deputy sheriffs that dogged his trail. Be hard for them to ever find the two of them in this maze of mountains and easy for him to avoid them if they tried. Perhaps a few moons spent with her in this high country would be soothing. He might even learn how to sleep again and not wake up at the first sound in the night.

"Let's go to bed," he said, thinking about her small body and the fire it contained. On his feet, he looked off to the southwest at the silhouette of the towering range that somewhere up there contained Red Elk's camp. *Dorothy, I'm coming for you.*

• • •

He left orders with Two Bird, if he didn't come back in a day, for her to load up Combs and take him back to civilization. She agreed, looking glum. The man was still asleep and they didn't bother to wake him. With that settled, Slocum swung aboard the roan and set out in the chilly first light of dawn. Red streaks topped the peaks. He pushed the roan through the stream and looked back for her. She stood on the bank waving after him. He gave her a salute, then turned his attention to the direction he must take and soon was in the tall timber.

The sun over the mountains in mid-morning, he set the roan on a pathway through the great trunks, where the distinct prints of a shod horse unmistakably a few days before had used the way. It could be Buddy's shoe prints. Feeling better about the whole thing, he pushed the roan in a long trot. Being aware and constantly looking for any telltale sign of the Apache, he studied the ground too. All signs looked to be over a day old, perhaps two. If the renegade had passed through there with her was all he cared about.

He reached the base of the mountain and studied the open trail that led skyward toward the gap he sought. Should he try to enter or wait until dark? For as far as he could see the trail held no cover as it cut across the barren yellow rocks and ground and disappeared over the lip and that too probably meant more open travel.

Weighing his chance, he sat and clapped the roan on the neck. Should he wait? At last his impatience ran out and he set the gelding up the mountain. He undid the trigger guard loop and drew the .45 twice to be certain it was ready, then jammed it back in the holster. If he was attacked, there would be little recourse; still, he needed to find the camp and, being a medicine man, Red Elk might expect his powers to protect him.

The roan surged up the steep trail. Slocum's right boot was in the stirrup grazing the side wall and his left was hanging over mid air. He kept a sharp eye at the ridges above him. Not much room to make a decision. If someone shot at him and he went off the roan's rump, the frightened pony might knock him off the ledge and a thousand feet into hell.

He wiped his sweaty palms on his pants' legs. Underneath each armpit his shirt was wet and the cool wind made it feel like icicles. When at last he topped out and glanced back at the spot were he started from, the giant timber looked like sprouts. From his vantage point, he could look back across the basin and speculate where Combs and Two Bird were located.

There was no smell of smoke, and the valley flattened and widened. Fed by a spring, somewhere higher, the small stream would fill a two-inch pipe, gurgling and splashing over rocks in a narrow cut. He found an opening in the brambles of berry canes that lined the banks to get through to water himself and the roan.

How far up this valley was Red Elk and his camp? Warily, he remounted and started southward, noting all the grass on the flatter ground and the timber that covered the steeper slopes. Red Elk could be anywhere in this country. Then he topped another rise and discovered that a small lake filled the basin. On the far shore, he spotted the tepee and smoke from a cooking fire. Where were the horses?

He slipped off the roan and hitched him out of sight in the trees. If this was his camp, where was Red Elk? The skin crawled on the back of Slocum's neck. He drew out the Winchester, and checked the chamber. Using the trees for cover, he went back for another look at the setup. Satisfied this must be the medicine man's lodge, he began to circle around the lake to get closer. Wind stirred the reflection of the mountain on the surface. No sign of a horse or any person.

He had hoped to recover the dun too. His bulldog mountain pony wasn't in sight. In a half run, he hurried to get close enough to see if the camp was inhabited. Out of breath, he knelt down fifty yards from the setup. Then an Indian woman came out of the tepee. She wasn't Dorothy.

Damn—had he came all this way for nothing? He checked around to be certain he was alone. Something was wrong here. No sign of any horses though a grassy meadow went back up the way. Was this someone else's camp and Red Elk's own farther up? He wiped the mustache of perspiration off his bristled upper lip. It was too far back to go and ask Two Bird. If this squaw saw him, she might spread the alarm. Nothing like being between a rock and a hard place.

Chapter 13

The charging lone Indian on horseback came out of nowhere.
With ear-shattering screams, the painted-face buck was bearing down on Slocum with his lance set to run it through him.
Slocum twisted; rising, he dropped the rifle and drew the Colt
as the dun horse's thundering hooves drew closer to him. In
a flash, he brought up the handgun and fired. The shot took
Apache, lance and all off the rump of the dun. He hit with
a thud on his back and laid still. Slocum jammed the Colt in
the holster and swept up the Winchester.

Talking softly, he walked down the dun, swung in the
good saddle and headed him for the tepee. The squaw saw
him coming and ran for the shelter. If Dorothy was in there,
she might go inside and kill her for revenge. He fired three
shots over her head. That dissuaded the Indian woman
enough that she turned instead and ran the other way. Slocum
slid Buddy into a hard stop, bailed off and stuck his head
inside the door flap. Seated cross-legged on the worn buffalo-
fur floor was Dorothy; her clothing filthier and more rum-
pled. He closed his eyes for a minute in gratitude.

"That you, Ruff?" she asked.

"Yes, come on," he said, then he rose and looked around
outside. No sign of anything or a threat.

"But I need to get my things—"

"No." He caught her by the arm. "We can get them later."

He loaded her on Buddy and then swung up behind her, still carrying the rifle.

"I need my divided skirt to ride like this," she complained.

Hell, ain't nothing but a coyote going to see your legs, woman. He reached past her and took the reins. "Hang on." He spanked Buddy on the butt with the rifle stock and sent him around the lake for the roan. They needed to get out of there and be quick about it.

Where was the Indian he shot? Nothing on the ground where that one fell. When they flew by the spot, he shook his head, tried to look for him, but was forced to turn back and guide the dun. At the roan, he jumped off and took her reins. He slapped the Winchester in the scabbard and unhitch him. In the saddle, he took one last look. Only the lake, no squaw, no war-painted warrior. He jerked the dun's reins up and prepared to leave.

"Hold tight," he warned her.

If she even heard him, he wasn't certain. But she could ride and he ducked some limbs. She did the same and he found the trail. In a short lope, he used the advantage of the valley floor. The long way off the mountain worried him more. They would be exposed on the trail with no way to hurry off of it in such a steep downhill drive.

Repeated times he looked back for any pursuit and also checked on her. No sign of any Apaches, and she seemed all right for the condition she was in. When he reached the brink, he tossed the reins over the dun's neck for her to guide him. She nodded numbly at his words for her to be careful. He felt satisfied the compact mountain horse could find his way down with or without her guidance.

Their iron shoes slid on the solid rock and forced the horses to scramble for their footing. He regretted leading the way, but they were already committed. With several thousand feet to fall, the horses repeated efforts to keep their footing made his heart stop. Slocum turned back repeatedly to be sure the dun and Dorothy were coming. The blankness in her eyes turned his stomach sour. She might as well have been flying. Outside of her natural ability to ride a horse, she was not with the living. He felt certain that she had retreated much more into her own world than when he first found her. No sign of the Apache on top; it was too much to ask for them to get off the mountain unscathed. He knew he had shot the buck who attacked him. Perhaps the bullet had been a dud. Not seeing him lying one on the ground bothered him—he looked again at the rim high above them. Nothing.

At last on the canyon floor, he felt a wave of relief sweep over him that left him cold. "Ride, girl," he said and crowded the roan in close.

If she heard him, he couldn't tell by her blank expression. "We have to ride hard, Dorothy. We have to ride hard!" he said even louder, hoping to break through the trance that held her.

"Oh, Ruff . . ."

His conscience hurt him, but he lashed the dun on the butt and hoped that she held on. She rocked, but acted glued in place when the gelding tore out down the canyon floor with him and the roan on his heels. It wasn't a time for the timid; they needed to move and move fast. Get back to camp, load up her husband and Two Bird and get out of these mountains. They had used up all their good luck getting to there.

He looked back, but saw nothing. Was this Apache some sort of god? A spirit? After he shot him, he figured that Red Elk was gone to the happy hunting ground. But the absence of the body worried him. Spirits were no problem, but flesh and blood were different. Lashing the dun on the butt sent him faster ahead, with Dorothy clinging to his mane, but able to sit him without a wobble.

The day was waning in the west; he dreaded crossing that next mountain in the dark. But it might be their only chance to get over it and head for the Rio Grande Gorge country. He daydreamed of being in a village and having enough guns ready to let him sleep comfortably. They were five days from that unless they ran their horses into the ground.

. They arrived in camp and he had to catch the dun's bridle to stop him. Two Bird rushed out, looked at her with her hand over her eyes against the bloody glare off the setting sun.

"How is he?" he asked the Indian woman in Spanish and nodded toward a shelter.

"Sleeping."

"Can he ride?"

Still looking at the numb-appearing woman on the lathered, hard-breathing dun, she shook her head. "He's too sick."

"What in the hell's wrong with him?" His impatience to be on the move and out of the mountains was eating hard at him. The longer they stayed the greater the threat of other Apaches finding them.

"He's still sick. This is her?" She nodded toward Dorothy, who was still seated on the horse and oblivious to both of them.

"Yes, that's her. I shot Red Elk, but he must still be alive. After I got her, he was not to be found."

She did not act surprised and that bothered him. Psychic— lots of women in the southwest had these skills and they saw things before they ever happened and knew things without being there.

"Is he alive?" he asked.

She shook her head. "I don't know."

"But you have an idea?"

She simply shrugged.

"Let's get her down then. We need to figure a way out of here." He looked at the dark, brooding mountain and shook his head. If Combs couldn't ride, how would they get him out? All that he needed was a sick man and his crazy wife, and the notion that Red Elk still might try to take her back. Two Bird took her off in the night to relieve her. They came back and Dorothy never showed any recognition, merely sat where the Indian woman showed her.

"I have food," Two Bird offered to Slocum. "I fed him some earlier. He sat up and ate it, but he is very weak."

"What's wrong with him?"

"He says his chest and arms hurt."

"Well. We sure aren't doctors." He filled his plate with the hot beans. Then he sat cross-legged on the ground and began to feed himself. Two Bird brought some to Dorothy, who had said little since they took her from the horse. Slocum looked up occasionally, but the woman did not act interested in the food.

"Here," Two Bird said in English. "You eat."

Dorothy never blinked, but did submit to her feeding her. She chewed like something mechanical and Slocum gave his nod of approval to Two Bird. The woman would starve to death if she didn't eat something. Then Two Bird made her drink and Dorothy looked so pitiful with the tin cup in both hands, the water dripping out of both sides of her mouth. Her entire state pained Slocum through the heart. She was much worse off than when he first found her. Had Red Elk done something to her? Or was it simply her retreat into the dark void of her mind to escape the horrible things that had been heaped upon her?

"What will we do?" Two Bird asked when she finished and wiped the woman's face.

Squatted beside him, the wariness in her dark eyes as she studied Dorothy, she told Slocum she was concerned and had no answer either.

Did she know how the whole thing would turn out? For certain she acted edgy about their condition. He felt itchy underneath his clothing.

"I will sleep beyond the camp in case that Red Elk tries to sneak upon us."

"He is shot?" she asked in Spanish, a language she conversed better in than English.

"I thought he would be dead."

"He is medicine man, they do not die easy."

"Bullets ain't choosy."

"I would come be with you?"

"No, you watch the camp and hoot like an owl if there is anyone or anything tries to come in here."

She nodded.

He smoked a roll-your-own cigarette. His first in days and he was grateful for the relaxation he felt from inhaling the smoke. Each puff was to be savored. He had no answer for their plight. Had his blow brought this on to Combs? Not likely, but the man needed to shut up that day.

"Where is my dog?" Dorothy asked, and caused him to blink at Two Bird.

"He's fine. He's at the cabin," he said so she would not get excited over the loss, though he could not recall any dog dead or alive at the place.

"His name is Jojo."

"Yes, Jojo," Slocum agreed, listening close to her.

"He's good company."

"I agree," Slocum said.

"I hope they feed him."

"They will."

"I saw those Indians take him."

"They did?"

Slocum exchanged a frown with Two Bird, who had not moved from where she squatted close to him. Then he shook his head, this was a new story.

"Oh, you saw them take him," she said as if they were not being serious with her over the matter. "You know he rode a painted horse. Apaches don't eat dogs, do they?"

"No!" both of them told her.

"Well, he sure took Jojo." She looked indignant at them.

Slocum shook his head. End of her conversation and he knew less than ever. Did the dog thief mean something or was it just passing through the empty space. When Combs awoke he would speak to him about this dog business.

"Time for bed," Slocum said to Dorothy and Two Bird went to help her.

He stood up and stretched; it would be a long night. He listened to the evening insects. Two Bird tucked her in and then came over to him.

"She speaks to spirits."

He nodded. Actually he feared she spoke to no one in this world and would never come back from the one she had eloped to. Even at the ranch, she was more in her own mind than was at the present. Whew. A sick husband, a crazy wife and a mountain range to cross with sixty bloodthirsty Apaches scouring the hills. He could have chosen a better place and deal.

In the early morning light, he returned to camp after a night of half sleeping and waking at every small sound. Two Bird was busy brushing the woman's black hair and plaiting it. Dorothy never looked up, never acknowledged his presence. He poured himself a cup of coffee. The hairdo made her look better than before with it hanging in her face. Two Bird had good ways.

Slocum squatted down on his boot heels and blew the steam from his coffee. He glanced toward the shelter where Combs slept. "He still alive?"

Two Bird stopped her hair fixing and looked in that direction, then she nodded. "He was up earlier. Not very strong."

Coffee in his hand, he turned to study the peachy first light crowning the peaks. He either needed to go for help or load them up and try to get them out. He looked back mildly as Dorothy began singing a lullaby. She had a lilting voice, and he savored the words, ". . . Oh, the green hills of home . . . I won't ever roam, oh, Johnny Dade."

"You no-good slut!"

Slocum turned and blinked at Combs standing with a gun in his hands. The man wore his pants and an underwear shirt, his galluses down, he did not look steady on his feet.

"Put the damn gun away!" Slocum shouted.

"I ought to kill you too. You probably been dipping in her like them Indians did."

"You don't know a damn thing. Put that damn gun up!"

"Hell, she's crazy. She needs killing."

"You put that gun up or you're going to die." The stupid devil would sure hurt someone if he pulled the trigger. His single-action Colt was already cocked. Unfazed by what was happening, Dorothy didn't even bother to look up at him.

Combs thrust the Colt threateningly at Slocum. "Listen, I ain't afraid of you—"

"You better save your strength for the trip over that mountain."

"She's a slut. A whore! She's screwed all them diseased Indians." He pointed the barrel at Dorothy, but he never saw Two Bird, who hit him over the head with a knot of wood. The pistol went off in the dirt. Combs' knees buckled and Slocum cringed at the report. That shot might bring the whole Jicarilla Apache tribe down on them. He rushed over and disarmed the moaning man.

He jerked him up on his knees by the arm. "We're loading up and if you can't sit in the saddle, I'm taking your ass out over that pass belly down. And one more trick like this and I'll leave you for the damn buzzards to pick. You savvy, Combs?"

"Yeah, yeah."

"Get the horses," he said to Two Bird. He looked around for Dorothy. Where had she gone? For crying out loud, she had been there one minute like a statue and gone the next. He stuck the man's Colt in his waistband.

He looked at the still-gray sky for some help. This whole thing had turned impossible.

Chapter 14

"Where did she go?" he shouted to Two Bird, who was leading up the horses.

"I'll find her," the Indian woman said, giving him the leads.

"She can't be far." Filled with impatience, he brought the animals up to be saddled. Two Bird fled for the bushes in a swirl of buckskin fringe. Slocum looked across the camp at Dorothy's husband. Combs would be no help, he sat on his butt holding the back of his head and moaning. With haste, Slocum began to pile on saddle blankets and kack, cinching them up and then the pack saddle. Where were those women? He took a fleeting glance around. No sign of them. How far did she go?

At last, he saw them coming back. He drew a sign of relief. Two Bird herded the much taller woman along, talking in small words, sounding soothing. She arrived with her ward and Slocum held the dun for Dorothy to mount.

"The shot," Two Bird said. "She thought we were being attacked."

Slocum nodded. "She's never seen Combs, has she? Here, I'll help you." He gave her a boast aboard the dun. Two Bird shook her head.

"You all right?" he asked Dorothy. If she heard him or his words registered, her facial expression never showed it.

93

Staring at the mountain, she said, "We better get out of here, Indians are coming."

"I can get on by myself." Combs gave him a scathing look.

"Good, but don't fall off. It'll be a thousand feet to the first rock outcropping," he said and let the man wallow his way on the horse.

"You take the roan and pack horse and go ahead, I'll walk," he said to Two Bird, drawing out the Winchester from the scabbard.

"I can walk—" Her dark face pained, she shook her head in disapproval.

"Go!" He pointed the way and led Dorothy's horse by the bridle until Buddy fell in behind the pack horse. Combs, looking bleary-eyed, ignored him and rode behind his wife.

Slocum gave a last look around. Were there Indians coming? Did a woman out of her head really know? No telling. He kept a wary lookout ahead and behind.

It would be one thing for him and one person, both well mounted, to escape these mountains, but with his entourage, it would take more than pure luck. By mid-morning, they reached the mountain base and the hard ascent ahead.

"Take a break," he shouted to Two Bird and she nodded. Slocum gave a glance back, saw nothing, then he hurried to help her get Dorothy off the horse.

Combs dismounted and, holding his arms close his body, stumbled off a few yards and with his back to them began to empty his bladder. Slocum steadied Dorothy on her feet. Two Bird was ready to lead her to the juniper thicket.

"Ruff, we need to leave here," Dorothy said under her breath.

"We will. Go with Two Bird now."

"So we're gone soon," she said.

"We will, Dorothy, we will."

"Do you have a milk cow?" she asked Two Bird. The Indian woman shook her head, leading her toward the brushy evergreens.

"I'm going to get one. We never have butter at our meals. Did you notice that . . ."

"She's gone plumb mad," Combs said. His eyes looked glazed over and he stood very unsteady.

"It's a tough climb ahead," Slocum said, ignoring the man's comments. "You up to it?"

"I'll make it."

Slocum turned his ear to a sound. Hoofbeats. "Two Bird, come on!" He turned to the pale-faced Combs. "Get mounted."

"What? What is it?"

"Riders. Get her on her horse and head up that trail. I'll hold them off."

Her brown eyes flew open. "We can't—"

"Get on the roan and you lead the way. I'll try to catch up later. You go on. Take them to civilization. Combs has money, he will pay you well." Dorothy was in the saddle, and he saw Combs was in too, but for how long would the man last?

Two Bird challenged him with a hard look.

"Get on that roan and go."

She relented and quickly mounted, trying to see the riders. She took the pack horse lead from him and booted the roan for the trail. He clapped Buddy on the butt and with Dorothy aboard, he surveyed the country for a sight of who was coming.

"You fighting Injuns by yourself?" Combs frowned at him.

"Get up the trail."

The man reined his horse around and followed the women. Two Bird was already well up the slope with the others behind her. The thicket should give him some cover; he headed for it. Still he could not see the riders. He watched the four horses cat-hopping up the mountainside and into the timber. Obviously the Indians saw them too, for they let out a war hoop. They burst into his sight. Five bucks stripped down to loinclothes and waving bows and rifles, intending to catch the escaping party.

Slocum took aim. His shot cut down the leader's paint horse. The rider went flying and the pony did a cartwheel. His shot also shied the rest left and right. He took careful aim and took another rider off his horse. Three to one, much better odds. Rifle butt in shoulder and ready, he watched them rein up their horse, looked at him in disbelief and whirled around. They galloped for the far ridge to escape the range of his .44/40.

"Now what do you want?" he asked aloud, wondering if they wanted him that bad. Indians could be fanatical or simply quit in the face of their losses; he'd seen them both ways. Usually though to charge into certain death, they needed a fanatical leader to show the way. These looked like youths, none resembling the buck he thought had been Red Elk.

One of them dismounted and dropped his loincloth, bent over and mooned him. The greatest insult an Indian could give his enemy. Slocum had seen the Comanches do it to defending buffalo hunters. He'd also seen some old sharpshooter, like Tatum, test the wind with a pinch of grass, set his sights and give the poor buck a lead enema with his .50 caliber Sharp's. Considering the distance, he decided to save his ammo.

In a Mexican standoff, they were holding a powwow two hundred yards away. Two Bird with her wards was getting higher up the mountain with each passing minute. The bucks appeared to be in no hurry, arguing amongst themselves loud enough that he could hear them, though he did not understand the words nor were they perfectly clear. Just guttural language.

If he survived until dark, then perhaps on foot he could try to get over the mountain. For the moment, he must defend this narrow strip that led to the top. The Apaches swiftly mounted and, screaming their war cries, charged three abreast at him.

He drew up the rifle, and through the V in the buckthorn sights, he drew a bead on the middle Indian's chest. The rifle's muzzle jumped up and the gun smoke swept his face. The buck threw his arms up and fell off his horse. The other two peeled off left and right. Slocum made one more shot at them, but he knew there was too much brush. Two for two.

Had they had enough? He hoped so. They could count three of their party as gone. None of the fallen stirred from where they lay. If no more came, then perhaps he stood a chance of surviving them. No telling, but he felt certain they would soon replace charge with stealth. That could be more deadly. He glanced at the timber on the mountain above him; no sign of the riders. He could only hope that they were headed for the pass on top. Be a heady place to be at that moment and not worrying how those bucks would try to get him.

No sounds, but the fleeting call of a raven. The cawing was like some spirit foretelling his fate in the vastness of the atmosphere. Like a bell ringer on a city street bringing news of some tragedy. "Hear ye, hear ye." Or a newspaper boy standing on a corner selling the latest edition with headlines. "Wanted man killed by Apaches!"

He'd seen and heard them all. No longer could he see any sign of the Indians. Obviously they were going to get together, but this time not in his sights. He couldn't blame them for that.

Would they quit?

No way to ascertain their next move, he slipped back to the junipers and took a seat on the ground. Part two would be the waiting game. He would not know for a while if they went back for reinforcements or at that moment were crawling toward him. That might be the toughest challenge yet for him. The wait had begun.

Small birds flittered in the branches. Their chatter and the wind's hush through the needles were the only sound. There would be no noise from the rawhide moccasins, the wearer would simply appear when at close range, knife or club in hand and charge at him.

Slocum considered the loose horses on the flat beyond. They grazed, raised their heads up and looked about, then returned to chomping on the grass. What were they looking for? Perhaps they would give away the location of the bucks stealing up on him. The pony with the most white on him raised his head up and sniffed the wind. His long mane flowed in the gathering breeze. Stallion-like, he curled his lip back, testing the air for the scent of a female, then he set his hind legs apart in preparation, and ran his huge spotted organ out. It quickly began to stiffen and swelled to elephant-size proportions with his efforts. He hunched his butt a few times and then he ejaculated a stream of foamy come. The huge hammer-headed prick strained a few more times to its utmost. Then it went from the size of a giant mushroom to a limp hose and disappeared. The stud gave a hard shake of his head and mane that he was satisfied he had bred the air anyway, and went back to grazing.

Besides the horny paint, nothing much happened as Slocum waited. Some ravens lit in a nearby pine tree, giving
him more encouragement that the Apaches might have left
the area, either to bring back more help or simply forget him.

The sun dropped lower in the west. Nothing. He tried to
sit still, but the skin crawled on his back. Closer to sundown
he would try for the paint stud. No telling if his scent might
spook the animal away. Many horse acted alarmed when they
smelled Indians and the reverse could be true for Indian ponies. Still the mostly white horse with only some small
patches of brown on his sides and hips looked like his best
bet as a way to escape.

The increasing wind worked in the Apaches' favor. It covered more noises. Still he couldn't be certain they had not
left the area. At last, he rose with care to his feet. Then, at
a low, run he worked his way to the edge of the thicket. The
horse never acted like he cared so far. The distance to the
stallion was perhaps a hundred feet. A stiff breeze rushed
through the juniper boughs. For a long while he considered
the open ground between him and the pony. Then, with re-
solve, he headed in a bent-over run for the horse.

The stallion raised his head, eyed him curiously, then lowered his muzzle to snatch off more grass. Stems and blades
sticking out of his lips, he again raised up as Slocum drew
closer. The eagle feather on the jaw bridle fluttered. If only
he could grasp the end of the rawhide rein that trailed to the
side. Rifle in his right hand, he bent down and scooped up
the rein in his left. The stallion shied. Slocum dropped the
long gun and used both hands to stem the animal's escape.

With great rollers coming out his nose, the horse gave him
a long snort. Slocum ignored his show and jerked him along
so he could recover the Winchester. Then in a bound he was
on the white one's back. He sent his heels into the horse's
side and they headed for the mountainside.

A figure rushed out of the juniper thicket, knife raised
high. How long had he been there? If he hadn't moved from
his place in the thicket—he might not be alive. No time to
shoot, Slocum knocked him aside with the Winchester and
sent the Apache sprawling. Then he shouted at the paint and
they tore up the steep grade in great cat-hopping jumps.

Powerful enough, he about unseated Slocum with each

hard lurch. But there was no way that the pony would shake his determined rider. Slocum looked back and saw in the growing twilight the Indian picking himself up. Too close for comfort. They would probably pursue him. He spanked the paint with his gun stock to go faster.

Twilight waned as he covered the final two hundred yards and reached the pass aboard the lathered, deep-breathing stud. Slocum slipped to the ground and dropped the rein, and he rushed back to the brink and tried to see any movement or pursuit in the deepening shadows. The strong wind swept his face. Nothing.

He turned and started for the paint. The sounds of iron shoes coming from the other direction made him whirl. Who could that be?

"Slocum? Slocum?" she called.

"Here." he said and hurried to meet Two Bird.

"Oh!" she cried and slid off the horse. She rushed over and hugged him around the waist. "I have been so worried about you."

"The others?"

"They are both asleep. Very tired from the hard ride."

"So am I, girl," he said and rocked her back and forth in his arms.

They made the camp and he hobbled both horses. Grateful for his own mount, he wished the paint had been gelded, but Apaches seldom castrated their animals. Still he knew the paint would want to fight their horses and try to cower them into submission. Despite his problems the pony sure beat walking up that mountain.

Two Bird fed Slocum some beans and jerky. He felt better but the antsy feeling had not left him.

"We must take turns guarding the way off the mountain?" she asked.

"I can—"

"I can help."

"Fine, you take the first watch and wake me."

She nodded. "The wind will soon lay so we can hear them coming."

"If they come at night."

"If they do."

Two Bird knew the Apache superstitions that kept many

Apaches from making war at night. Still even she didn't trust them not overcoming some of those misgivings for their own purposes. Slocum nodded as he chewed the last of the peppery jerky. It would be a night to be aware.

Chapter 15

Ravens served to awaken him. The insides of his legs complained from riding bareback. He also found some unused muscles that stiffened while he slept. She had a small fire and he could smell the strong coffee. He needed a stout cup of it to clear his head. In the first light, he strapped on his holster. Combs' gun in his saddlebags he would reload for his own usage before they prepared to leave. Crazy man anyway, why did he want to kill her? She hadn't invited them bucks to that gang bang that he felt certain had happened to her when they killed Ruff and burned the main cabin.

He squatted beside Two Bird, who sat on her heels at the fire.

"They're still asleep?" he motioned to the two in their blankets on each side of the fire.

"Sleep good when tired."

"We better get them up. Two days and we'll be in civilization and get both of them off our hands."

She agreed.

"Didn't hear or see anything on the mountain."

"No."

"Neither did I. Good, I'll saddle the horses."

Two Bird knew a shortcut to the road. Slocum agreed. Combs wrapped himself in a blanket after some grumbling and managed to get on his horse. The man no doubt was sick, but the only way he'd get better was medical attention.

There wasn't any in these mountains that Slocum knew about. Dorothy went through the motions as if in a dream state and Slocum soon had her on her horse. His string lined out, he bounded on the paint and brought up the rear.

The road she spoke of was the one that eventually would end at Espanola. The route wound down from the hot springs at Pagosa in Colorado to the Rio Grande River crossing below the main gorge. A good dip in the smelly hot springs might drive some of the stiffness from his body. But they were miles to the north and he wanted shed of the Combses. Espanola was the place to do that.

Midday they reached the wagon road. Slocum had considered the problems and chances they took using the route. Chances for raids by the hostiles would be much greater; they must be watching the road for a chance at a small, defenseless band of travelers. Still he wanted both Combses off his hands and the sooner the better. Milton was no better health wise and his frame of mind soured with each passing day over his own appraisal of his poor wife's choice of who she was raped by. Dorothy could have been on the moon for what she knew about anything.

"Take the road," he said and pointed to the bare ruts that wound southward. He glanced north, saw nothing and followed after the groaning Combs.

"Can't we stop?" the man asked.

"And get killed? No, thanks," Slocum said and waved for Two Bird to continue.

"These horses must need to graze," Combs protested.

"They can in Espanola." Then he pushed past the man and joined Two Bird. "You know a place to camp this afternoon off the road?"

"Yes. Halfway to Espanola."

"Good, we will push for there. Let's trot. I'll lead Dorothy's horse." He took the reins and set both the stud and Buddy in a trot.

Her blank expression haunted him. Though she sat the dun all right, she was not there mentally with them. Didn't even know her own husband. Things were bad, and he hoped that someone could help her.

They made camp in late afternoon. It was at a spring and the best they could do, Slocum felt. The horses all hobbled and put out, Slocum went back to camp. Combs, wrapped in a blanket despite the warm air, had fallen asleep with his back to a log.

Seated cross-legged on the ground, Dorothy combed her black hair. She acted as preoccupied as ever in her own little world. Two Bird was busy making a small fire and nodded to him.

He dug out a small cigar from his vest and struck a match on the back of his pants' leg. On the second drag, he heard riders and some bells and bounded to his feet.

"Who is it?" she hissed.

"White men, I would say. Indians ain't that loud."

He saw them coming up the trail from the road. Buckskin clad and under wide brimmed hats, they looked like traders or trappers with rifles in the crooks of their arms. The count was three.

He felt Two Bird pull on his sleeve. "Bad hombres," she said with a frown.

"You know them?"

"Yes, very bad."

"Howdy there, my name's Epple. My friends call me Cather," the big man on the black horse said. Across his lap rode a Winchester in a beaded buckskin case. "Why, darling, don't I know you?" He frowned at Two Bird.

She shook her head, but Slocum realized she wasn't looking up at the gray, bearded man.

"Old Cather'll remember ya, maybe after while, darling. I may have to jerk off them leggings and look at her bare ass though to do it." He threw back his head and laughed aloud. The other two joined in his hilarity.

The older one on the right looked past sixty and the one on the left in his twenties.

"Mister, Cather don't never forget what their butt looks like," the youngest said, between his amusement, balancing a Spencer over his leg.

"That's Huey," Epple said. "This here's Pappy. Why, he's bred more squaws than any man living, ain't ya, Pap?"

"Damn look hard at him, mister, what's your name? Why I'd bet you've seen a hundred half-breeds look just like old Pap." Huey pointed his Spencer at the older man.

"Slocum's mine." He felt an itching under his shirtsleeves.

These men were all she said they were. With Dorothy in her present state and Combs no help to him, he would have to ease these boar hogs out of camp somehow without an incident.

"What's wrong with her?" Epple asked with a frown as he stared at Dorothy.

"She's a victim of an Indian raid. Taking her to the doctor. That's her husband, Milton Combs. He's been sick."

"Gawdamn, she's good looking." Epple stepped off of his horse and walked over. He knelt down and put his finger under her chin and raised her blank face up.

"Hello, darling." She never looked at him. A smile cracked his bearded face. "She's plumb tetched."

"Leave her alone," Slocum ordered.

The Spencer clicked and Huey's threat cut the air. "Get back. Cather gets what pussy he wants."

Slocum's heart stopped. He had to keep down the rage inside his chest. These bastards were the scum of the earth and he had to choose between dying or watching them torture Dorothy. Two Bird came and hugged him.

"Don't—"

"You are, oh, so right, little squaw," Epple said and the grin of a madman crossed his bushy face. "Get back and you take his gun out of that holster. Careful, little one. You both could be killed in one shot." When she removed Slocum's handgun and dropped it, Epple waved them back.

"That old man over there, he's your old man, huh, darling?" he asked Dorothy.

No response from her. Combs blinked his rheumy eyes as if he had been sound asleep. He closed one to try and see the outlaws from the other one. Beads of sweat ran down his face and Combs' pallor looked snow white.

"What do you want with her?" he asked like a drunk, his words slurred. His head rolled slightly as he spoke.

"I want to screw her."

"Huh!" Combs grunted. "You may as well, every gawdamn Indian did."

"Stay put, Slocum," Huey warned. The younger man's attention obviously had not diverted to Combs, who sat with his back to the log.

"What's her name?" Epple asked.

"Dorothy."

"Dorothy? Dorothy? You and I are going to play a little game." He reached over and began to unbutton the front of her dress. "We're going to play a little game, darling."

She never acted like anything was happening. Slocum could see the excitement dance in Epple's blue eyes as he worked to undress her. The outlaw was getting worked up. He soon had the dress open and peeled it back. Her pear-shaped breasts were exposed and whiteness of her skin was stark as he fondled them.

"Hot damn, darling, you are something."

Huey came over and moved Slocum back a few feet with the barrel of the Spencer. "Don't try nothing foolish."

"Leave her alone, Epple," Slocum said, despite the threat of the boy and his rifle. "She ain't in her right mind."

"Oh, I think she is." He unbuttoned his belt with the gun holster and several knife sheaths to set it aside. Then he gently pushed Dorothy down on her back and smiled again at Slocum. "You can watch or close your eyes, big man."

He sorted her legs apart and moved between them, talking softly to her like a man did to a loose horse he wanted to catch. He dropped his gaze down to the black triangle and shook his head. "Man. Oh, man, this is pretty."

Slocum saw that her blue eyes had never wavered from when Epple started until that moment. Dorothy wasn't in this world. She had no idea of her plight.

Sitting on his heels, Epple raised up, untied the lacing on his leather pants, shoved them down below his hairy butt and sat back to stroke his pecker. His humming grew louder.

Where was Two Bird? Slocum dared not act too interested in her. Strange. Somehow the small woman had slipped away from them. Good, she would not have to suffer a similar fate. He checked on Pappy, who was licking his lips as he watched Epple bring up his erection, who then parted her legs and moved to stick it in her.

"Darling, darling, you're ready, I guess—"

"Oh, Ruff, hurry, he'll be coming home—" Her words cut off.

Slocum knew by the way Epple's butt plunged that he was inside of her.

"You no-good bitch! You screwed that cowboy too."
Combs was on his feet and kicking at her.

"Get that bastard back!" Epple said, having to rear up to
stop his attack and push Combs back.

Pap threw his arms around Combs and dragged him away,
kicking and cussing.

"Tie him up!" Epple shouted and grasped his slick dick to
reinsert it. "Gawdamn him!"

Pap and Combs wrestled some and then Combs passed out
on the outlaw. Slocum wondered if it was for good. He hated
worse Dorothy's babbling at Epple as he screwed her. She
arched her back and cried out in pleasure as the outlaw's
hairy butt pounded her harder.

All that Slocum could think about was how badly he
wanted his bare hands on those bastards. How much he
wanted his hands on his gun. Huey kept reminding him to
stand still with the muzzle of the Spencer in his gut. He heard
Dorothy's words to her lover, her grunts and groans and at
last he knew by the roaring growl that Epple had come. They
fell in a pile.

Epple raised up and smiled as he used part of the tail of
her tattered dress to wipe off his slick dick. He rose and
laughed. "That old man was crazy, wasn't he? Cared more
about her fucking the hired man than me doing it."

"He dead, Pappy?" Huey asked.

"Naw. But he sure fainted."

"You boys can have that little Indian wench. This Dorothy
is mine."

"Where did she go?" Huey asked, trying to see around
Slocum.

"She get away?" Epple cried. "Damn it, you'll have to
jack off till we find her."

"Where did she go, Slocum?"

"Don't ask me. One minute she was here, the next she's
gone."

"Pappy, you go look for her," Epple ordered.

"Hell, she's a damn Apache, you won't find her," the old
man grumbled as he headed off in the growing darkness.

"She won't go far. She's got a meal ticket here."

"Bullshit!" the older man swore, going off in the twilight.
Epple pulled up his pants and retied them. Then he shifted

his balls around, and shook each leg. "Well. My, my, guess I'll have to dress her. Can't have them tits sticking out all the time. Make old Huey here and Pap jealous."

He knelt down and pulled the dress together. Then he buttoned it down a ways. "You get to my camp, you can walk around naked, darling. Here it might make them horny." He laughed at his own joke.

Pap returned. "She ain't out there."

"Hell, you ain't even looked. All right, fix some food." Then he eyed Slocum as if contemplating what he must do about him. "Tie him up real good."

"Be glad to. She that good?" Huey asked.

"Don't get no damn ideas. She's the boss's pussy. I get through with her, you can have her."

"I'll be ready," Huey said, tying Slocum's hands behind his back and making the rope cut deep into his skin.

"Where did that little Indian bitch go?"

"Damned if I know, maybe to get her brothers to come down here and scalp you three."

"You're a tough smart ass, Slocum. I get tired of your mouth I may stick a .45 in your lips and blow you away."

For a second, Slocum considered telling him to try that; then he reconsidered. He needed to stay alive and kill each one these rotten outlaws. Rape a demented woman; at least she had some sense about her when he had her. She and Ruff must have had quite an affair. Now her husband knew all about it; all he probably wanted to know about it. He should have stayed home more instead of going off and leaving two warm-blooded young people there alone.

Was Combs dead? No, he saw him move a little. A heckuva mess to be into; he strained at the binds behind his back. Pap put some meat that he brought in a skillet and heated water to cook some rice too. No telling what else. Where was Two Bird? He hoped she hadn't gone home. No telling, but he figured she'd come back and try to help him escape. He hoped so anyway.

The outlaws never offered to feed Slocum when they ate. During the meal, Combs came around and mumbled his words until Huey got up, went over and kicked him. That shut him up.

Out in the night, a coyote yipped at the stars. Slocum

turned to listen, uncertain if it was an animal or human making the sound. That was all they needed, an Indian attack. Apaches never did much after sundown; but they were never this desperate before either. The ropes burned his wrists from straining at them.

He had turned off the conversation from amongst the outlaws. Epple bragged about his exploits. The other two tried to match him. Everything about the situation made Slocum want to gag as his empty stomach drew tighter. They sure better kill him before they left or he would search the earth for their worthless hides.

Dawn finally cracked the distant range. Through his lack-of-sleep-gritted eyes, he watched the outlaws loading his things with theirs. They had the roan horse, Buddy and Combs' sorrel, but he never noticed the bay pack horse or the paint stallion. Perhaps Two Bird took them; he could hold out for that anyway. He had sat up all night, dozing a little, then awakening to try and figure a way to escape his binds without success. His arms were too stiff from being bound to be of any use if he was free.

"Well, Slocum, I'd gut shoot you, but that would waste a bullet. I figure with you on foot in this country, no food, no horses, you might last a couple of days before you became buzzard bait," Epple said, then he threw his head back and laughed. "Sure do appreciate you bringing me Dorothy here. I'll take good care of her."

Slocum could see they had her on a horse. He read the emptiness in her eyes, the black hair in her face, uncombed and the light wind tossing it. Rather than risk the ire of the outlaw he remained stone silent. His deepest desire was to someday look down the barrel of a Colt at this outlaw. *God protect her.*

Chapter 16

The outlaws were hardly gone when Slocum discovered they had left his saddle. It lay across the empty camp where he had left it. Strange that the outlaws had missed it, but in their haste to leave and still in the half-light they must have over-looked it. He knew they took most all the supplies and packs. There were no movements over where Combs lay on his side. The man was either passed out or silent.

"Combs?" he hissed, but the man made no reply.

Slocum scooted over on his butt to a rock outcropping and began to try to rub the rope in two on the sharpest edge he could find. The sawing action caused the hemp to bite deeper into his skin. It didn't matter; he was going to get free. Time was of the essence.

Deeply absorbed in his effort to get free, he saw movement in the junipers. He stopped and sat up, then he smiled as Two Bird rushed over brandishing a knife.

"They are gone," she whispered in his ear and laid a hand on his shoulder as she cut loose his binds.

"Thank God," he said in relief, working his stiff limbs and at last getting to his feet. She went over to free Combs. Slocum turned his back to vent his swollen bladder. So tight with pressure, the flow wouldn't start, then at last the stream burst forth. Why, with that force, he could have pissed clear across the Grand Canyon. He thought it never would end.

Slocum went to his saddle and dropped on his knees to

open the bags. In his hand he soon hefted Combs' Colt. Carefully he checked the chambers; four cartridges was all it had. Combs had shot one. Slocum's further search found no more ammunition in the pouches. They were all on his holster belt that the outlaws carried off with his revolver.

"Slocum," she hissed and broke into his thoughts about the shortage of ammo.

He rose, stuck the pistol in his waistband and went to where she was with Combs. The man sat on his butt, with his back against a log. Something was wrong, the right side of his face looked different. The corner of his mouth sagged and his right arm looked useless.

Slocum squatted down beside her. "What's wrong?"

"I can't use my arm," Combs mumbled and indicated his right side. "My leg either."

"What's wrong with them?"

"I don't know."

Slocum and Two Bird exchanged a frown. No way that Combs could ever ride out of there in his condition. Yet there was nothing Slocum or the Indian woman could do for him. There might be help—should they go north or south? Colorado was a good hundred miles one way and Espanola that far south. Either way they faced the threat of the renegade Apaches. Standing, he let out a slow exhale. Instead of taking the outlaws' trail, he had to get a sick man to a doctor. They would go north. After they left Combs with some medical person they could go find that worthless Epple's lair.

"Horses?" he asked her.

"Two."

"You did good. Where are they?"

"I can go get them."

"Fine. I'll get him some water. Oh, look for poles."

"Poles?"

"Poles for a travois. To carry him."

She nodded she understood and ran off in a flurry of buckskin fringe. Slocum only took a minute to watch her, then he turned back. He hoped that she would find some; if they had to cut down a tree with a knife they would be all day.

She returned on horseback, riding the paint and leading the bay. The horses hitched to a juniper, she hurried over to where Slocum was trying to give Combs a drink. Most of it dribbled down his chin. The alarming weakness in the man shocked him.

"I can do that," she said. "I saw some poles back there on the trail."

He nodded and left her to water Combs. He soon found the gray, weathered sticks she meant. They must have been discarded tepee poles. Slocum knew the Jicarilla used that form of shelter like the Plains Indians did, while the other Apaches in the southwest used grass wickiups. These were dry, cracked and ancient, but maybe they would work with a blanket stretched over them to haul Combs. He hoped so as he shouldered them and started back for camp.

At last the travois was hitched to the bay horse and the patient put on the travois. Two Bird bounded on the bay's back. Slocum rode the paint bareback since they needed the saddle to secure the rig to the bay. They began the trek north. The hiss of the poles rang in Slocum's ear. It would be a long way to Colorado. And they had no food, save a few crackers and dried cheese from his saddlebags. It might be a long time before they ate again.

The road entered a canyon, when she shouted, "Wait!"

Slocum turned and looked back. She slipped off the bay, dropped the rein and rushed off into the bushes. What was she doing? He rode over and, frowning, peered into the brush where she was beating something with a pine knot club.

"Porcupine!" she said proudly.

Slocum nodded. He had feasted on the spiny beast before in another emergency. Old mountain men would never kill one of the slow, lumbering creatures; they said the quilled critters were the only thing a desperate man could hunt down as food when he was without a weapon.

Time to stop and eat.

While she did the painstaking job of skinning it, Slocum gathered wood and built a fire. He made Combs comfortable. The man had no use of his right side. He had to be supported and half carried; he also had fell into deep depression and spoke little. The critter was soon roasted.

The gamy-tasting meat was hardly enough for three people and Combs had trouble chewing his, but did get some nourishment down. Slocum checked the sun; they had some hours left to travel. At this rate they would be a week getting to

Colorado. He shook his head as he bellied up on the paint.

They made camp at sundown. They were deep in the mountains and they used a small meadow for the horses to graze. All the three humans had for supper was the memory of the porcupine. Slocum didn't know what the next day would bring, but their plight would grow serious.

They set out in early morning. Good things to eat ran through Slocum's mind. Great beef roasts, prime rib of elk, lavish meals at the home on the plantation as a boy. Roasted pig with an apple in his mouth. The road soon joined a small stream and Slocum looked at the green walnuts, wishing they were ripe enough to furnish the rich, tasty kernels of the nuts. Then he reined up the paint.

"Walnuts," he said and turned to look at her.

She wrinkled her nose at him like he had gone crazy.

"No, get me all the green walnuts. We need them all."

She shrugged and leaped off the horse. Soon she had a mound of them gathered, and he brought a sack towel and put them in it. He climbed down the steep boulder-strewn bank, with a wave at her to join him. Seated on the small stream bank, he removed his socks and boots. The water would be cold.

"What are you doing?" she asked.

"Green walnuts will stun the fish. You go down there and catch them. Throw them on the bank."

With a scowl of disbelieve, she went down to the slower pool and removed her moccasins and leggings. He wanted to laugh for he knew his plan would work if there were any trout in the stream. A shiver ran up his back when he stepped in the icy water. No matter, he began to swish the sack of green hulls back and forth in the stream.

He nodded to reassure her as he kept up his sweeping. She stood naked to the waist, knee deep with her hands on her hips. He had begun to tire of the exercise and had started to doubt even his own wisdom when she shouted and threw a silver-bodied fish on the bank. Then another and she was busy, the fish turning up their bellies. He waded downstream to help her. They would eat again.

"Plenty good way to fish," she said, excited.

He agreed, catching an elusive ten-incher and tossing it on the beach of sparkling flippers.

They ate fire-cooked fish until they were full and packed the rest in his saddlebags. At midday, they set out. Slocum trying to accept the fact they needed to get the dull, half-paralyzed man to help. Combs ate some fish and that made Slocum think perhaps he was improved, but there was no real answer. The sooner they got him to medical care the better it would be. Slocum felt certain that someone would stake him to some supplies and ammunition to go after Epple.

At dark, they camped in a great grassy basin. He made Combs as comfortable as he could in his bedroll. The man barely spoke and so when in his cracked voice he called out, "Slocum," he turned on his heel in the twilight and looked back at the man.

"Them bastards never got my money—"

"Don't worry about it," Slocum said, squatting down beside him.

"It's in my boots—"

"Good, you'll need it."

"Anything happens to—me. I want you to have it."

"You don't owe me anything."

Combs tried to rise up. "I want you to have it!"

"All right, don't get so worked up. Ain't nothing wrong with you that a doctor can't fix." He laid the man back down.

"Slocum, you could have left me back there. I'd have left you if you were in my shape."

"I doubt it."

"I don't . . ."

Slocum had been saving a half of a small cigar. His cigarette makings used up, he went to the fire and sat down cross-legged. The orange-and-blue blaze consumed the dry wood with tongue-like flames. The strong, acrid smoke filled his nose. He lighted the cigar off a burning stick and tossed it back in the fire when the cigar came to life.

"He talked to you," she said, taking a seat beside him.

"He's worried about dying."

"You think he will die?"

"I don't know. I'm not a doctor. May not be anything that they could even do for him."

She acknowledged his words with a bob of her head. "When we find this doctor, then what will you do?"

"Go and kill Epple."

"I will ride with you."

"It will be dangerous."

Her amusement began as a giggle, then she threw her head back and laughed aloud. She clapped him on the leg. "It has been that way since you caught me in the berry patch."

At daybreak, he heard it: the clucking of some wild turkeys. He caught the white horse and leaped on his back. He eased him across the knee-deep grassland and rounded a bend to see a large flock of gobblers on the hillside. They acted undeterred by his approach, busy feeding on grasshoppers in the grass. He picked out a large hen within pistol range and one shot downed her to a flopping wad of feathers as the others left in a loud clap of wings.

He rode back to camp and held up his prize. "Lunch today."

She ran over and took the bird from him. It was hard for her to hold it high enough to keep the bird's head off the ground as she admired it. Then with a nod of approval she went to skinning it.

They soon loaded Combs on the travois and were underway. Slocum had ran the cylinder around so it was over an open chamber and he had three bullets left. But they had a turkey to cook for their midday meal and still several smoked fish in his saddlebags.

The day would have went well, except before midday one of the dry poles cracked and broke, spilling poor Combs in the road dust. They reined up and Slocum rushed back to check on the patient.

"You all right?" Slocum asked, helping get the man on the bedroll that she had unfurled.

"I'll be fine," Combs said with a cracked voice. The pallor of his face and the man's shrunken eyes did not have the appearance of someone *fine*.

Slocum felt deep concern for Combs as he stood up, removed his hat and began to scratch his head. In the great basin they were in, it was over two miles in any direction to the timber and he had no ax or saw.

"I'll go look for a new pole," he said to her when she completed covering Combs and straightened up.

"I will watch him," she said.

"What will happen next?" Slocum asked and shook his head.

His search for a suitable pole began when he reached the edge of the forest. Rotten ones were strewed about, too heavy trunks for him to use and he pushed the painted stallion though the boughs and up the hillside. He needed an old lodge pole of some sort. His looking reminded him of the search for the needle in a haystack story.

After several hours, he managed to find a gray, weathered one that looked strong enough and suitable. It was wedged in a jam he was forced to unstack, and then he had to hand drag the ten-foot-long pole up the sheer mountainside to where he left the stallion tied. At last on the horse's back, he dragged it behind the paint and they started back. The sun was setting fast and all he could think about was the smoked fish they would have to eat.

The next day they traveled northward at the pace of the travois hissing on the ground and reached a stream by late afternoon. His green walnuts technique produced several larger trout. By sundown, they were full of fresh fish and turkey, and even Combs looked stronger sitting up.

Slocum wished for a smoke, but with his supply depleted, he would have to wait for a chance to bum or buy one. He watched the small flames lick at the stick of dry wood. Heat radiate in his face as the coolness of night began to settle in.

"I owe you my life. . . ." Combs' voice was cracked and dry as he sat braced with his back to a tree trunk.

Slocum shook his head. His hardheadedness to recover Combs' wife had put them in the situation that they were in. Then again, he never expected to meet up with someone like the outlaw Epple—Epple would pay the price. Where was Dorothy? Damn, she didn't deserve that rutting boar.

Chapter 17

The days dragged on. Fish, porcupine, and a hungry day thrown in, Slocum dared not spend another shell and anyway no game Slocum spotted was close enough for a sure kill. He felt grateful no raiding parties had found them. But the lack of traffic on the road also concerned him that Indian trouble wasn't over. Usually there would be freight wagons and pack trains going back and forth. But through the sixth day that they traveled, they had seen no one.

Mid-morning on the seventh, he saw yellow guidons snapping in the wind and blue uniforms—a troop of cavalry coming out of the north. He turned back to her and indicated the patrol. "Soldiers."

Damn yankees never looked so fine in all his life as they did. He dismounted heavily and kept his arms over the paint's back to support himself.

"Where you guys come from?" a whiskered scout with mid-south accent asked, dropping off his pony and coming over to Slocum.

He looked the buckskin-clad man over and shook his head. "Hell."

"You're lucky as pejeepers to be alive. Them Apaches have painted their asses red and sure are on the warpath. How did you get through? Army's got the road stopped on both ends. They attacked and burned two wagon trains north of Espanola."

"Who are you?" a shavetail asked.

"My name's Slocum." He remained slouched over the paint's back and looked the young men over. "You got a doctor? I've got a man back there ain't faring well."

"Shot?" the officer asked and dismounted.

"No, sick."

"My name's McFarren. You came from out of there?" He glanced over at Slocum as they walked to the travois.

"Yes."

"That an Apache horse?"

"Yes, we held off an attack. That's how I got the horse."

"Lucky man." McFarren knelt beside Combs, whose eyes were closed. The officer felt for his pulse. He frowned and shook his head. "I'm sorry, this man is dead."

"Dead? Damn, he was talking not an hour ago." Slocum straightened up and looked in dismay at Combs' lifeless body. All that work and still they lost him. Well, Combs, it looks like your grave will line the road to Pagosa Springs.

"He did not want to die in his boots," she said in Spanish and began to take them off.

"What did she say?" McFarren asked.

"Oh, he asked not to be buried in his boots and willed them to me." Slocum recalled Comb's words about his money, but would have forgotten if she hadn't remembered, and they'd been planted with him.

"Fine, I can have my men prepare a grave."

"I would appreciate that."

"Sergeant, assign a detail to dig a grave for this poor fellow."

"Yes, sir." The noncom rode back to get the men.

"Well, Slocum, you must have had quite an adventure getting here?"

"We did. You ever heard of an outlaw called Epple?"

The man shook his head.

"He kidnapped Combs' wife a week ago. Left us all to die and hadn't been for Two Bird there, we would have. Combs must have had a stroke. We've being hauling him for a week to get this far. They didn't leave us much either."

"What could I get you?"

"If you had a cigar you could spare. . . ." He rubbed his calloused palm over his whisker-stubbled mouth; the notion

McFarren might have one made the saliva flow behind his teeth.

"Certainly."

The troopers began to spade up the sod. McFarren went to his saddlebags and produced two, he handed both to Slocum.

"Hey, I can pay you."

"No, my gift. Tell me what you know about the Apaches." Both men squatted down, the scout knelt down using his Sharp's as a support for his right arm. McFarren waved over his noncom. "Slocum is going to fill us in."

"Red Elk kidnapped Mrs. Combs in an attack on a trading post . . ." Slocum began telling the whole episode to the men. He pointed to the places where things happened on the map that the officer produced. Showed them the camp where he found Two Bird and described the Apaches' hunger plight he learned from Two Bird.

"Sorry Indian agents stealing the things intended for the Indians are more than half the problem. Them buying sorry supplies when the government pays for the best. Then the white men invade their reservations. I understand their problems," McFarren said. "Still, we need to get these warriors under control."

Slocum agreed as he chewed and smoked on half of the cigar. He planned to save the rest for later.

The grave was completed. The sergeant gave Slocum all the man's valuables. A watch, jackknife, gold chain, ten twenty-dollar gold coins and fifty dollars in paper money. Combs' body, wrapped in a blanket, was placed in the fresh-smelling hole and a few words were read over him before the soldiers covered him up. While they were halted, the troopers had taken the time to also cook some food and they offered some to Slocum and her.

Their bacon and beans tasted like great food to Slocum. He hoped he never ate another gamy-tasting porcupine ever again. After his second plateful, he retired with her to a place away from the troopers.

"Where will we go?" she asked.

" 'Pagosa Springs. Get some supplies, horses—" He looked around to be certain that in the growing darkness they were alone. "You look in his boots?"

She shook her head, then stood up and ran to the bay horse to untie them from the strings. She rushed back to him, hugging them.

They were made-to-fit boots and he ran his hand down in them. Good boot, real fine leather, then he started feeling in the seam of the vamp. There was a wallet-like slit in them and he could feel the edge of crisp bills. Combs' money would finance their recovery of his wife. Slocum found the same in the other boot. He nodded to her.

"All we need to do now is find Epple. You know where he hides?"

"No."

He reached over and drew her to him. "We will find him," he whispered in her ear as he held her tight in his arms. "We will find him."

Some folks called the field of sulfurous-stinking springs a page from hell. When Slocum reined up the paint stallion before them, he took a different look. He thought the yellow and orange piles of residue looked like heaven's gate. The false front row of wooden-framed businesses that sat on the edge of the great patch of boiling cauldrons appeared to him to be civilization in its finest form, and even in its crudest conception, it reminded him again of their hard-fought efforts to get there.

"Well, Two Bird, we're here."

He dismounted in front of the hitch rail. The sign hand-painted on the small glass front window said Cafe. He hitched the paint and she tied the bay to the rack.

"We're going inside and have us some real food."

She wrinkled her nose and shook her head. "I'll wait here."

"No, there are no demons in there." He pushed her toward the door, reached past and opened the latch.

"No squaws in here!" someone shouted.

"She's with me," Slocum said flatly.

Halfway down the counter, the red-faced man raised up on his toes, looked them over and frowned. "Oh, all right," he finally relented and the grizzly-faced stool sitters turned to look at them too.

Slocum showed her a chair at a small table. She sat down with her hands in her lap and her gaze downcast. In that pose she looked hardly more than a child. He gave her wink when she looked up, but it did not instill much confidence in her.

"What'll it be?"

"You got some meat and potatoes?"

"Elk steak and potatoes I got."

"Two plates and two coffees."

"I don't usually let—"

"I know, you don't let Indians to come in here." And with that said, Slocum indicated to the man he was excused.

The waiter turned on his heel and went toward the back. Several of the men at the counter grumbled at him, but the waiter ignored them too. Slocum considered the Colt in his waistband. He had three cartridges in the chamber. That was all. When they left the cafe he planned to buy another holster and plenty of ammo.

A gray-whiskered, toothless man stopped and stared at her. "She yours, mister?"

"That's Two Bird," Slocum said.

"Ha, best pussy I ever had in my life was Injun, mister. Yes, siree. You want to sell her?" His coal-black eyes glared hard at Slocum.

"No."

"I'd give ya a good, fair price for her."

Slocum shook his head.

"Don't blame you. I had her, I won't sell her either."

"Wait before you go," Slocum caught the ragged sleeve of the man's coat. "I'm looking for buckskinner who calls himself Epple. You ever heard of him?"

The man made a sharp nod of his head that he knew him. "You don't want nothing to do with him, mister."

"You know where he is?"

"No. But his henchman Huey is down in the French Palace Bar drunk as hooter's goat right now."

"You sure?"

"Hell, I told you so."

"Thanks."

"Watch yourself. He's a back shooter and a claim jumper."

"Epple around town?"

The man shook his head and looked out the corner of his eye to check and be certain no one was close enough to overhear them. "Got to go."

"Thanks."

"Ain't no thanks for me. Them two are bad medicine. Don't say I didn't warn you."

"I won't," Slocum said, and the waiter brought their food.

Considering their plates of food, he nodded to the man they were all right. Deep in his own thoughts, he decided his next stop would be the gunsmith. He'd seen the sign up the street. Huey was there in Pagosa Springs. Where was his boss and the older man Pappy?

"Go ahead and eat," he said under his breath to Two Bird, who had not touched a thing on her plate.

She nodded obediently and picked up the spoon.

He nodded in approval. Huey was only a hundred yards away. It would tax him to eat the delicious-smelling meal and sit there. There would be plenty of time for the outlaw.

Chapter 18

A shot rang out from down the street. Slocum stood on the boardwalk in front of the cafe, picking his teeth.

"Stay here," he said to her and began to run. The ruckus was at the saloon marked the French Palace. Several of the dance hall girls, hysterically screaming, had run outside into the street. They huddled in the center of the dirt road and peered fearfully back at the swinging doors. Gun smoke began to boil out over them.

Slocum reached the front window and could see over the green half curtain that the place was fogged up with gun smoke and couldn't make out anything inside. Then a barkeep in a white apron burst out bat-wing doors coughing his head off.

"It's all over, folks," he said, still choked by the fumes. "Just a misunderstanding between two gamblers."

A man who ran up looked official, dressed in a black suit and hat. His silver star pinned on the vest was barely exposed as he questioned the barkeep.

"Huey was his name," the barkeep said. "Went for his gun and O'Leary shot him with his derringer at face-to-face range."

The lawman frowned with impatience. "This Huey dead?"

"Wasn't moving when I saw him last in all the smoke. Guess his gun went off too when O'Leary shot him."

"Huey who?"

"Marshal, mind if I go and see about the dead man?" Slocum asked.

"It's your life, you're risking it going in there."

"Where's O'Leary?" Slocum asked, prepared to enter the swinging doors.

"He went out the back way."

"Hold your fire," Slocum said to whoever was inside and parted the doors. He spotted a pair of boots, toes turned up, and crossed over to them.

Squatted on his heels, the acrid smoke burning his eyes, he looked over the outlaw. "Can you hear me, Huey? You got one chance—you hear me?" He jerked the boy up by his lapel. The cloth grasped tight in his fists, the outlaw's head lolled to the side. For a second, he thought he was too late.

"What?" Huey slurred.

"Where's Epple?"

"Goose Lake . . ."

"He still got Dorothy Combs?"

An evil grin exposed the kid's yellow, tobacco-stained teeth. Then he spoke, "He's still fucking her too." He giggled. "He's—" Then the youth went limp in his hands. His eyes turned to stone and stared at the tin ceiling tiles as the smoke began to thin out. Slocum lowered him to the floor.

"Learn anything?" the marshal asked.

"Him and an outlaw named Epple kidnapped a white woman over a week ago. I wanted to know where his partner was at."

"He tell you?"

Slocum stood up and nodded.

"Where?"

"He said Goose Lake."

"South of here. Not many folks come back from there that go in there uninvited."

"I've got an engraved one."

"What's that?"

"An engraved invitation to Goose Lake."

"All that I can say, mister, is be careful."

"I will." He nodded to the lawman and then he crossed the barroom, pushed the swinging doors aside and walked out into the pine-scented air. He would be very careful. *Fooled once, all right, fooled twice, shame on you.* He considered that old adage as Two Bird rushed up and hugged his waist.

"I'm fine," he assured her. Only he had learned the location of the outlaw he sought. Epple was at Goose Lake. And with Dorothy. He herded Two Bird across the street toward the gun shop. That would be his next stop. His pockets filled with Combs' money, he needed a good handgun and rifle. That would be the start.

"I've got a new .44 Colt," the big man said, standing behind the glass case. "Cost you fifteen bucks. Some folks really like them because the cartridges interchange with the .44/40 Winchesters."

Slocum nodded and the man took the revolver out and laid it on the counter. He picked up the oily-smelling weapon and took aim at a bucket hung on a nail on the side wall.

"That your squaw?" the gunsmith asked.

Slocum nodded, opened the loading gate and turned the cylinder on his left forearm to check each cylinder.

"She Apache?"

"Yes." The gun would do what he wanted and the man had good point, the same ammo fit a rifle.

"There's folks around here would string her up."

"Two Bird?" Slocum frowned and then he glanced at her. "You got ammo?"

"Sure, you want a whole box?"

"I may need it in case they try."

"They would," the gunsmith continued. "They sure hate them."

Slocum shoved a bullet in the first cylinder, clicked it over to number two. "Why? She ain't done nothing to them."

"Yeah, but nits breed more nits."

"Killing breeds more killing too."

"You have a point. You need a rifle to go with it?"

"How much?"

"New, twenty-seven, and used ones are sixteen."

"Better take a new one. You got a scabbard?"

"Four bucks."

"Anyone ever complain how high priced you were?"

"No, 'cept you."

"That holster and belt?" Slocum indicated the one on the nail overhead.

"That's got lots of nice work on it."

"I just need to pack a gun in it."

"Two bucks. I gave a cowboy five for it."

Slocum doubted in reality that the man had given more than fifty cents for the holster. "Throw in another box of shells and I'll pay you." He didn't have time to argue much longer. Thought of Dorothy's plight in the hands of the outlaw stabbed him hard. Huey's last words stuck in his mind too. The dying outlaw's haunting giggles—he deserved to die.

After paying the man, Slocum filled the gun belt with cartridges. When he turned and looked out the front window of the narrow shop, he noted several men in the street. They looked as if they had a purpose. He paused and considered the short Indian woman beside him.

"Is there a back way out of here?" he asked the gunsmith busy cleaning his hands on a ragged flour sack.

"Yeah, why?" Then the man blinked, obviously seeing the crowd in the street. "I don't want no trouble—"

"Then get the hell out of the way." Slocum brushed him aside with the Winchester in the scabbard as he caught her by the arm and headed for the rear door. He turned in time to see the gunsmith rush to the front door.

"Him and her's going out the back way!"

Slocum gritted his teeth. He considered firing a shot at the no account worthless outfit, instead he shoved her out in the alley. They both began to run. He pointed to a narrow space between two store buildings. He checked that there was no sign of any of them yet in the alleyway, then followed her down the opening. Close to the street, he could see their horses hitched at the rack.

The clatter of boots on the boardwalk and breathless men running made him hold her up. "Wait."

"Sumbitch—" one man panted going by them.

"They went behind—" the other one huffed.

Slocum dared to peek past her. Those two were going the other way, backs to them.

"Get on your horse," he said as they broke and ran for their mounts. "You ride on, regardless what happens to me."

They were in the saddle in a flash and lashing their horses to escape. She led the way and he dared to look back. It would take them some precious time to saddle mounts and take up the chase. He wasn't taking a chance and pointed her south.

Disappointed over the fact they had no supplies, at least he had guns and ammunition enough to survive. He would still need some directions to this Goose Lake. Somehow he would find the place, but he still regretted having to run off back there. No sign of pursuit. Like so many mobs, they fast lost interest when things grew difficult for them. Still, the hatred for Indians was instilled in them; it would be hard for both sides to exist when the war was over. Warily, he shook his head. Two Bird sure had not hurt them—she had been starving except for the berries she picked. They could care less.

He reined up in a grove of junipers and let the hot horses breathe. Then he studied their back trail, because the fact he couldn't see them meant nothing. They still could be coming.

"What was wrong with them?" she asked in Spanish.

"Loco," he said and shook his head. No need to tell her that they were out to kill her, she knew it well enough.

"Muy loco."

"Si."

"You know where this Goose Lake is?"

She looked at him hard as if in deep thought, then shook her head.

"Apaches probably call it something else," he said and tossed his head for her to ride on.

They rode in a hard trot southwestward. Slocum spotted some smoke. It looked like chimney trace and he headed toward it. When they topped the next ridge, the corrals and outbuildings came into view, and the source of the telltale sign rose from a stone fireplace on the side of a low-walled cabin.

He reined up short and gave a call. "Hello, the house."

The door cracked and rifle barrel came first. The stern-faced woman in her forties bearing the rifle looked them over with sharp eyes. Straight-backed, with her dark hair pulled into a bun, she looked lithe but also all business in her starched white shirt and divided denim skirt.

"What's your business up here, stranger?"

"Looking for Goose Lake."

"It ain't here."

"Wait, ma'am. We don't want anything except some directions."

"This is my ranch."

"We know that. We won't be a here a second longer. Can you even tell us where Goose Lake is?"

"Why?" She blinked her diamond-hard eyes at him.

"An outlaw is holding a white woman captive up there."

"Hmm," she snorted out of her thin nose. "What you going to do about it?"

"Try to get her out."

"Well, since you're such a damn fool, I hadn't ought to even tell you. You got next of kin I should notify?"

"No, ma'am."

"See them two peaks in the west?"

"Yes."

"Hell and Goose Lake are on the other side."

"I'm obliged, ma'am."

"You know Epple?"

"We tangled once."

She nodded as if considering his words. "Then you know who you're up against."

"Pappy up there too?"

"I guess."

"A gambler got Huey."

"There's more riffraff up there too. Hard cases all the time cutting through here on the run. Keep your back to the wall, mister."

"Slocum."

"Martha Kline."

"Pleased to meet ya."

"Yeah, sure, I maybe the last white woman you ever see. Good day, Slocum."

"I'm obliged."

She shook her head in disapproval and went back inside.

He reined his horse around and tossed his head toward the distant range. "You ever been up in those mountains?"

Two Bird nodded.

"You recall the lake?"

"*Si.*"

"That's Goose Lake. I figure."

"Apaches call it 'Place of Dead Bear.' "

The notion struck him. First, Apaches revered the bear, second, they seldom spoke of the dead. For them to call it by such a name meant one thing to him: they didn't like the place either. It would make an ideal place for an outlaw like Epple to hide out. Not to be bothered by the red men or the white.

He glanced back over his shoulder. Martha Kline was a cold woman. She had to be tough to live up there. Did she have a man? He guessed her to be in her forties. No sign of children about the place. A lot of unanswered questions for him to ponder as they rode southwest toward the place of *Oso Muerto*.

Chapter 19

In late afternoon, he shot a small mule deer with the rifle. With the deer's body tossed over his saddle in front of him, they rode on. Along a flush stream short of the range, he decided to camp and hung the deer in a pine tree for her. She quickly skinned it and then they weighted down the carcass in the stream to cool it, save for the back strap and liver that she cooked over a low fire.

Horses hobbled for the night, he joined her. Seated cross-legged on his bedroll, he smoked half a cigar. Shame he hadn't had time to buy more along with the supplies they needed. Their rations would be the venison until they found better. His mouth watered at the prospect of the fire-flavored meat, as the melting grease dripped on the flames, caused the fire to sizzle and flair up occasionally.

Poor Combs, he reflected. He must have gone mad in the end. Wanting to kill his poor wife for the Indians raping her to hide his shame or perhaps his own inability to penetrate her. Women seldom went looking for it if they received enough attention at home. Then those heart attacks or whatever finally took Combs' life. Maybe if he had not come along with them, he'd have lived longer. No telling. Then, over the mountains, there was Epple and Dorothy to be concerned about.

Slocum studied the stars and inhaled the hot smoke. It filled his lungs and he exhaled slowlike. The nicotine filtered

129

into his bloodstream and eased him. What happened to Red Elk? Dead men did not get up when they were shot. He glanced at Two Bird squatting by the small fire. The red light danced on her copper face and the highlights glistened like gold in a dark pan. After they ate, he would see about her. A fascination with his thoughts about the small, muscular body under her buckskins began to arouse him.

Again he drew on the cigar and the end lit red. The smoke, following the same route, settled and eased him further, except for the growing need he felt for her. By the time they finished eating he would sure be ready.

The meal filled him and stopped the gnawing hunger in his belly. She sat beside him and looked up. He nodded to her. She quickly smiled and nodded back. Then she bound to her feet in the growing darkness and shed her leather leggings, exposing her short, shapely legs. Then she bent over and began to remove the buckskin dress over her head, exposing her shapely butt in the process until at last she stood with her dress on her arms. Slowlike she pulled it off her arms. Her small, hard breasts shook as she shed the garment. The coal-dark nipples grew more pointed.

He nodded in approval at the sight before him. He pulled off his boots and let the cool night air strike his bare feet as he stuck his socks in them. Then he rose, still staring at the slight rise to her stomach with her deep-set navel and beneath it the dark triangle of her pubic hair.

When he shed his pants, she moved in and undid the buttons of his underwear. Before he could slip the shoulders of it off, her small hand cuddled his scrotum and the other teased his stiffening dick. He stepped out of his underwear and she knelt down before him. In an instant her lips closed over the head of his dick and he rose on his toes to escape the desperate excitement that grasped him.

He shut his eyes to savor her attention. His erection increased with each exciting second. Her fingers gently rocked his sack and the tender contents as she continued to suck on the burning head. Her tongue's action encircling the ring sent shivers of electricity up his spine and in bolt-like flashes through his butt.

His hands cradled her head, the hard braids in his grip. He soared with eagles. Until at last he could stand no more and gently pulled her upward to disengage her volcano mouth. Then they both lay down on the bedroll. The cool wind swept over them, but neither noticed the temperature, except their own and it was fiery.

With her lying on her back with his knees between her parted legs, he soon began to part her gates with his taut dick. His glans ached with the skintight throbbing that pulsed like a time bomb. He drove it deeper and deeper. She placed her heels on the backs of his knees and arched her back to move against him with a fury. The contraction she caused only added to his aching wand as he pounded her harder and faster with each drive.

She moaned and threw her head back with newfound effort. Her fingernails dug into his back and all he could think about was the explosion he sought. The maddening drive to seek relief grew to a new crescendo. Harder and harder he poured it to her, the tighter she grew inside. Until her muscular force began to strangle his prick's very existence, then he felt the head swell to new pain-filled dimensions and he strove it to the bottom of her well.

From the depths of each testicle rose the hot lava; it began the journey out of the tiny tubes and through the prostrate like a freight train that shot flaming arrows into his buttocks. It exploded, coming out like a Fourth of July rocket.

She screamed at that very moment and hunched herself hard against him. They both collapsed in pile, out of breath, out of the world and spent. His bleary eyes searched the night and save a coyote's yelping, there was nothing looked out of place. They climbed under his blankets and slept with their naked bodies nested in a ball until before dawn.

When they awoke, she soon discovered his boner and in a moment was on her back under him. This time they copulated with more restrain and she even laughed aloud, then shook her head.

"Too much," she said, then wrinkled her nose at him.

"Never." He felt himself begin to be aroused in the flank.

Quickly she arched her back and the forces tightened on his tool. The contractions of her muscled walls began to work on him. Then he felt the gathering explosion and shoved it deep into her for the shot. His gun went off. She settled into a dreamy pile and smiled at him.

"You have a very lazy squaw," she said and closed her eyes as if going back to sleep.

"That's okay," he said and got up to go pee. "She's very good for other things."

He could have sworn she blushed at his compliment. The cooler morning air sweeping his skin, he pissed away his tender erection. Perhaps in another day they would locate the outlaw's lair. Anyway, he hoped so. Then, with a shudder in the peachy first light of sunrise, he hurried back to dress.

After breakfast, he saddled horses while she cut back the venison to the hind quarters to carry, and they prepared to leave. When he climbed aboard, he could see the divide between the ranges and wondered what he would find up there and on the other side. No telling, he booted his horse into a trot and she followed.

"This place ahead. Is it hard to enter?"

"You ride over a pass."

He held up his hand he understood. So they must scale a range and then drop into the Goose Lake side.

"How many ways in?" He twisted to look at her.

She shrugged. "Maybe one, two. I only know you must ride over the mountains to get there."

They rode out of the grassy flats and into the timber by mid-morning. Tall firs with their frosty-looking boughs rose above them. The trail showed some signs of activity, but nothing looked expressly fresh. Still, Epple could have ridden hard for his lair and been over this way days before. Or he could have entered by another route. The next problem they faced—did Epple have guards posted or lookouts? No telling, but this was the "land of no return," according to many folks, so he better be prepared for everything.

What was Huey doing up there in a card game? Perhaps the boy was there to keep an eye out for any other threat to the man's stronghold. No telling. The one sure thing was that Huey would not do anything, but stare at the dirt tossed in on him for the next eternity.

They climbed the trail upward until they topped out in a bare, granite-strewn V. The way proved narrow and an eagle screamed his warning at them. The shrill scream reverberated and echoed in the confines. He twisted in his saddle and she nodded in approval. They must be going the right way.

"He likes us," she said of the eagle.

"Good thing that you read him that way. I thought he was pissed at us being here."

She shook her head. "He is our friend."

"We need him," he said and turned back around.

The clunk of their horses' hooves on the rocks sounded too loud, but there was nothing he could do about it. In this crevice, they were simple targets. He would be glad when they were back in the shelter of the tall timber. At last they rode out of the pass and in the distance he could see the kidney-shaped emerald lake far below.

He nodded to her and she responded in approval. No sign of any guards or lookouts, but they had a long descent before them. If Epple was down there, they needed to be very careful and not alert him. How? Rest in the timber and let nightfall take them. He could better avoid detection and scout them out in the cover of darkness. When they reached a bench, he indicated they would go aside.

The way into the dead and strewed timber was hard, but they soon found an open spot and dismounted.

"We will leave the horses here," he said to her.

"Saddled?"

"Yes, we may need them to escape quickly."

She agreed.

So he drew out the rifle and they began to descend the mountain through the timber, forced to climb over downed trunks and entanglements of fallen branches. The going proved slow, but Slocum felt certain that if they rode in they would alert Epple long before they ever reached him.

By late afternoon, they had reached the bottom and were scouting above the lake's edge for the hideout. He heard a horse whinny and nodded to her that they must be close. She hurried to be closer behind him. Pausing, he studied the open ground ahead they must cross when they left the security of the timber. The brown, shortgrass-covered ridge offered them no cover. Time to either go on or double back and try to find another way. With a deep sigh, he headed for the scrub evergreens a hundred yards away. Bent low and running he was out of breath when they reached them. They worked their way through the clogged bushes and at last, he smelled smoke.

They couldn't be far. He bellied down and removed his hat to better see beyond the lip of the ridge. The ring of axes also came to him and he shared a nod with her as she joined him. Beneath them, he saw a handful of men, mostly Mexicans working to split firewood with axes and doing camp chores. The horse herd was in the south grazing on the flats; they looked unattended. Several wall-sided tents were set up, but he could not see anyone familiar besides the workers.

Where was Epple or Dorothy?

With the pungent piney smell in his nose, he lay on his belly considering his next move. Wait until dark, then try to locate her. The Mexicans looked more like workers than outlaws, but they could still be fierce. He needed Dorothy out of there and as quickly as possible.

What if her and Epple were not even in the camp? They might be somewhere else. Bellied down on the ridge, the notion bothered him too. All this effort and he might not even be on the outlaw's camp. Still, there had to be some kind of clue, for these men to stay up there; they had to have a source of funds. They obviously were not miners or ranch hands. This had to be Epple's camp.

It would be hours till sundown; his stomach complained about hunger. They both would have to wait.

"I could run off their horses," she said. "Then you could rush down and see if she is there."

"Both of us getting away might be part two."

She wrinkled her nose at him. "I could ride one back and get you."

"What about her?"

"I see."

He yawned wide. "This won't be easy."

"Look!"

He focused on the figure coming out of a tent. Was it Dorothy? Wrapped in a blanket, he could hardly make out much about the person. He watched her disappear around the tent, then reappear, but going away from him, he couldn't be certain. The individual disappeared in a small grove of junipers.

"Was that her?" Two Bird asked.

"I'm not certain."

"How will we know?"

"Sit tight. We don't need that bunch down there to sound an alarm that we're here."

"I could go down there like a lost squaw."

He shook his head. "No. All that horny bunch down there would rape you."

She gave a shudder of her shoulders under the buckskin blouse, then she nodded she understood his concern.

There was no sign of the person in the blanket coming back from the thicket. He fidgeted with some twigs as he waited. If only he knew she was in that camp. Epple could have taken her off somewhere for his own purposes—no telling.

Then he saw the older man they called Pappy ride up. He came from the south, so there must be a way out of the basin in that direction too. At least there would be his tracks to follow if they needed to leave that way.

Pappy dismounted, removed his weather-beaten hat and scratched the thin, gray hair. Then he undid the cinch, dropped the saddle and turned the pony loose to join the others. The bay went and rolled in the dust, gratefully. Pappy stretched and then went inside a tent.

Where had the old man been? Lots of questions that Slocum couldn't answer from the ridge. No sign of the figure who went in the brush either. They must be constipated or on other business. He studied the blue lake water over the small hill from the camp. A few resident geese and some loons piled the sides. He nodded as Two Bird rose and indicated she was going back to the animals.

Too many things he didn't know. Where Epple was or Dorothy's location. Perhaps dark would bring the answers. He hoped so.

Chapter 20

A mournful coyote's song serenaded the stars. Slocum started for the camp by going down the backside of the hill. In the night's cooling air, he could make out forms of the conifers and low sagebrush. The pungent smell of the evergreens filled his nose. Some of the rosin from the sticks still clung to his fingers, making them sticky to the touch.

The last of their instrumental music making had subsided and the camp looked asleep before he began his descent from the back side. He hoped he found the woman alive. No telling what he would find; there had been no sign of either her or Epple. The figure in the blanket had never reappeared. If it had been Dorothy, they would have been looking for her, he felt certain. Still, this amounted to a strange camp of men—no women in sight. Mexican men usually had women along with them to do the chores like split wood and cook. This was all done by men in this camp. Not even a few Indian whores hung around there. They worked such places where there was food and usually whiskey was available, money being secondary to most of them.

So without any female company, they were up in the bowels of the mountains, doing what? Answering to Epple and on his payroll? If he didn't find the chieftain there, where would he be? All these things floated about in his mind as he moved stealthily toward the camp hoping to find the poor woman and extract her from their midst.

He came low around the corral. Pappy had entered the middle tent. Slocum squatted on his heels outside the tent and listened to some snoring. Hearing one man's nasal growling, he felt certain he had the right one and slipped to the front. A quick check about the place and he eased himself inside. A few moments to allow his eyes to adjust he could make out the man sleeping on a cot.

From behind his back, he drew a razor-sharp hunting knife and stepped lightly until he was beside the sleeping outlaw. He laid his knife on the man's neck. Pappy jumped awake.

"Who—"

"Keep your voice down or have your throat slit."

"Gawd—yeah, what . . . do . . . you want?"

"Where's Epple?"

"I don't—" Slocum increased the pressure of the blade on his skin. "All right, he's got a camp on the hill south of here."

"How far away?"

"Couple miles to the south—get that knife off me. It's cutting me."

"Get up and put your boots on. One move and you're dead."

"I understand." Pappy gulped.

"You better."

The man pulled his boots on and rose slowlike in his one-piece underwear. Slocum checked outside and then shoved his prisoner out in the night. He was ready for any trick, but the man acted subdued and marched ahead. Pappy presented a real problem. If he let him loose he would wake up the camp; if he kept him, he became his responsibility. Slocum glanced back—no movement. Bad as he hated the old man, he couldn't kill him in cold blood. They'd tie him up and go find Epple. He looked off to the southwest and dark jagged lines of the mountains; he wondered how far Epple's camp was from there.

He'd learn soon enough.

She had the horses cinched up and ready. They tied the grumbling Pappy to a pine trunk and he complained as Slocum went to gag him.

"What if no one finds me?"

"You chose this life, not me." He put the gag in place and then they rode out.

Slocum was careful. He went wide of the horse herd, figuring there would be horses in Epple's camp to take her out on. Probably some of his own. Like the roan and Buddy who were not in the camp herd.

He used a cupped match to check the prints in the dust. Each time after he figured out the tracks, he swiftly blew them out. And they went on up the trail. The cavernous darkness of the timber forced them to rely on their horses' senses. Several times they lost their way and had to backtrack.

His eyelids heavy with fatigue, he dismounted and tried to study the open country ahead. If Epple was camped in this meadow, he could not make it out in the pearly starlight.

Then a coyote cried and another answered. She pushed her horse up beside him and grasped his sleeve.

"Apaches."

"You sure?" he whispered.

"Yes."

He turned an ear to listen for the sounds in the shadowy valley. Another yip came from the timber on the west and he agreed with her ascertainment. Apaches at night on the prowl or were they getting ready for the sunup? He checked the Big Dipper and decided it would only be a half hour away. Were they after Epple too? Obviously they weren't there for tobacco, what most beggar Indians usually asked for. Should he warn Epple? No chance of that and surviving if there were very many bucks out there.

Who were they? He eased the Winchester out of the scabbard and stepped down. He motioned for her to come forward.

"How many do you guess are here?"

"Several. There are five over there."

Five? Whew, he felt lucky they had not ridden into the setup. If there were five on the west, then the party on the east must be double the number from their yips. Where was Epple's camp? It must be further down the long, open meadow. The next yip told him that was where the war party was headed. He swallowed hard. Was it their plan to take the woman or merely kill Epple and her? Only time would tell.

They must wait in the dark confines of the timber, keep their horses quiet and wait.

Sunrise finally began and on signal the screams of the attacking warriors began. Few shots were fired and soon the long file of bare-chested riders began to parade down the meadow. Slocum and her backed into the timber; hearing the bragging bucks and their dancing ponies on the ground as they headed for the other camp. Then Slocum made out a familiar figure on a roan horse leading a white woman on a dun— Red Elk. No doubt the blank-faced woman was Dorothy, who looked hollow-cheeked and tired. It sickened him; no doubt her treatment at the hands of Epple had been severe.

"Son of a bitch," he swore to himself. Then he turned to smother any nicker from his horse. He could only hope, in their jubilance, that the Apaches ignored their tracks of the night before.

"What will we do?" she asked when the war party at last was gone from earshot.

"Go see if there is any food left at Epple's camp."

She agreed with bob of her head.

They found some jerky not contaminated in the wreckage of the camp. Epple's demise proved to be an ugly sight. His mutilation was hard even for Slocum to more than glance at in passing. He felt no great grief over the outlaw's passage, but the severe way he died and was treated made a knot in his throat as he chewed on the peppery jerky.

"They will attack the other camp," she said.

"They're not my worry. I came for the woman. Red Elk has her again and there's nothing I can do to stop him."

"What will we do?"

"Go back to get supplies, then go and look for him. He is medicine man who hopes to learn from her. We will find his camp again."

She nodded. "Can we go back—"

"No, not Pagosa Springs, they hate Indians. We'll have to find another place." He shoved the rifle in the scabbard, drew up his cinch and then swung aboard. "Do you tire of my wandering?"

"No." And she smiled warmly. "Better than picking berries for my food."

In the late afternoon, they rode through the smoking ruins of the camp. Men's bodies were filled with arrows, stripped of their clothing and looked stark in the scarlet blood from mutilation. The Apaches' worn-out and cripple ponies were left behind and replaced by the fresh ones from the herd. Acrid smoke of the burning canvas and log sides filled the air and swept his eyes as he rode through the death and destruction. No need to look close—there were no survivors. They found nothing to eat and headed up the mountain.

The gagged Pappy stood where they had left him, still tethered to the tree, when they rode up. The dark crotch of his underwear told the story of him pissing in his pants.

"You're a lucky man," Slocum said and reached down to cut his binds. The old man fell on his butt and struggled to remove the gag.

"Whatcha mean?"

"Apaches got the rest of them. Guess they weren't looking or they'd have found you."

"Huh?"

"You hear their war cries?" He scowled at the man.

"Thought it was crows and they were shooting at them."

"It wasn't. They got Epple and everyone in the main camp."

"They killed Epple?" He scowled at Slocum until he nodded in reply. Then he shook his head in belief. "Them red bastards."

"Ain't much difference," Slocum said and swung his horse around. "Red or white. Guess you can find your way out." Slocum motioned toward the mountain pass for her.

"Wait! You can't leave me here!" the older man cried out.

"Oh, what's the law?" He shook his head in disapproval, motioned for her to ignore him and ride on.

They crossed over the pass and were far down the other side before darkness forced them to halt and eat more of the jerky. Seated on a great log, he considered what they must do next. Would Red Elk go back to his sacred mountain? More than likely. They still had enough of Combs' money. Best they headed up into Colorado, found a more friendly town or outpost, got a pack horse and some more supplies. They sure didn't need to try Pagosa Springs again.

Somewhere in the night, a coyote yipped and he smiled to himself. It was a real one.

• • •

Three days later, they reined up and studied a crossroads. He could make out a trading post ranch with corrals. Slocum rubbed the stubble around his mouth on his calloused palm. What were the odds they hated Indians? Perhaps he should make her stay up there out of sight—in case—it would be a good idea.

"I'll go down there, buy a pack horse, some supplies. You wait here."

She agreed and he booted his horse off the hillside. Through the timber, he could hear someone shooing horses. He placed the shooer in a dark slab-built shed behind the main building. The dark smoke of their forge's fire snaked skyward. Slocum swayed from side to side in the saddle as his horse came off the steep hillside. Busy making a mental list of what supplies they needed, he hoped to be in and out of there in a matter of minutes. Money counted big in isolated places like this, where people's main income from their stock of things came from trading for furs and farm produce of locals.

The storekeeper was standing behind the small bar at the side of the room, waiting on two grizzly-faced men in fringed buckskin who turned and looked blandly at him, then turned back to their drinks. Slocum glanced over the small stock on hand and stepped to the counter.

"Be right there."

Slocum signalled he heard him, being in no hurry. The tall, black-bearded man in the stained white apron came over and asked what he needed.

"Coffee, flour, baking powder, rice, tea—"

"Man, wait. Take me a minute to find all that," the storekeeper said, hurrying toward the back and opening the door. "Clare, get in here. We got a customer."

"Now, what all?"

"Coffee."

"Name's Milt Ricketts. That's my wife, Clare." He gave a head toss as a woman twenty years his junior in her late twenties came in the open back door. She patted the loose brown hair down on the side of her head. Obviously a lot younger than her husband, she shooed him toward the bar. Ricketts went without protest and the drinkers ordered more whiskey when he reached them.

"You're passing through?" she asked, sacking the coffee beans in a small poke.

"Yes, ma'am. Ten pounds of flour."

"Ten pounds of flour?" she asked, sneaking looks at him the whole time she weighted up the white, fluffy meal.

"That'll be enough."

"You prospecting?" She finished the flour project and reached on her toes for the can of baking powder. Looking at her nice, slender figure in the dark-blue checkered dress, Slocum speculated on what she would look like undressed. A long derriere and pear-shaped breasts under the dress would be interesting enough. Ricketts was lucky to have such a lovely wife in this wilderness, especially a young one.

"No, just passing through. Ten pounds of dry beans."

She nodded and dipped them out of a large sack. "What else?" she asked with a smile.

"I could use a pack horse. Apaches stole mine a couple days ago."

"Stole your pack horse and didn't get you?" one of the buckskinners at the bar asked.

Slocum nodded.

"You're damn fortunate to be alive." The man shook his head.

"Show him that bay horse," Ricketts said to her.

She agreed with only a small bob of her head. "This way," she said and led him out the back, past her fresh wash on the line. The horse shooer nodded at them in passing. A lanky boy of perhaps twenty, bare to the waist overalls, sweat ran down his suntanned chest.

"That's Billy, my husband's son. Milt was married before," she said as if she wanted to explain. They reached the corral and he peered at the long-headed bay.

"How old is he?"

"Nineteen."

"The horse?"

"No, Billy." She gave him an I-don't-know look concerning the animal.

Slocum climbed over the fence and hemmed the horse up, caught him, checked his teeth and decided he was six or seven without any splints or ring bone on his legs. Sound enough for his purposes. If they weren't too high, the pony would do for a pack animal; he acted well.

"How much?" he asked, climbing over the fence.

"Oh," she said as if taken from her dreams. "You better ask my husband that."

"He sent you out here. . . ."

She blushed and then chewed on her lower lip. For a moment, he thought she would say something, but she didn't. They headed back for the post. She glanced back again at the youth bent over nailing on a shoe. Then she led the way inside.

"You want him?" Ricketts asked.

"A blanket, a pack saddle, halter and lead and him?"

"Cost thirty bucks."

"Ten," Slocum said.

He noticed the buckskinners followed the woman's movements to her place behind the counter.

"I need twenty for him."

"Twelve dollars, hard cash."

"Damn," Ricketts swore. "All right, but you're cheating me. Help him load up after you figure his bill, Clare." Then he turned back to the other two and then began to laugh about something else.

"It'll be fifteen dollars with the twelve-dollar horse and rig," she said, looking up from her figures on the brown paper.

He dug enough money from his jeans pockets to pay her. She counted it and nodded in approval. Then she took down a homemade halter and offered it to him. He went to the corral, caught the horse and led him to the back door. Slocum knew something was eating at her; she might never tell him, but he felt it. She brought out a Navajo blanket and handed it to him. He brushed the dirt and hay off the pony's back and put it in place. Next she delivered the cross buck saddle. With it cinched up, she bought out the first pannier and her blue eyes met his.

She was silent. Still he knew she wanted to talk to him in private. He could hear the other three inside laughing and getting drunk. She brought out an armload of his purchases.

"You have a woman?" she asked in a soft whisper.

"Yes, why?"

"I would go with you—if you needed me."

"But you're his wife?"

"There's going to be trouble—him and that boy—"

"Over you?"

She nodded. "I need out of here." Quickly, she checked around to be certain they were alone, then hurriedly put the items in the pannier. Without another word, she went back inside.

Slocum buckled the straps down on the one she had filled. It bothered him to leave a woman who'd asked for his help— but she was Rickett's wife. What kind of triangle had developed between her and the boy and her husband? Obviously one that she figured would soon explode.

He considered Dorothy and her plight, Two Bird on the mountain above him who the whites wanted to lynch and her own people who didn't have any food. We've all got problems, lady. No way that he could help her. He shook his head to dismiss even the notion.

She hurried down the back steps and filled the empty pannier. "You're a good man, Slocum. I saw that right off." She struggled to strap it down. "You think about me. You can do something, you come back and if it ain't too late—" She checked around. "I'll go with you, wherever you want me too."

"Obliged," he said and tipped his hat to her. He led the bay around in front and unhitch his own horse. They had the supplies they would need to track down Red Elk. He glanced at the open door and saw her standing there expressionless and he nodded again. Then he left.

He headed up the mountain, the sluggish-acting bay coming behind. Finally he reached the bench on the side of the mountain and reined up. Two Bird rode out of a thick stand of conifers and shook her head in disapproval.

"Two riders are coming after you." She motioned with a toss of her braids at his back trail.

Slocum pounded his palm on the saddle horn. "Damn the luck."

Chapter 21

Was it pure coincidence or on purpose they were on his back trail? Those two buckskinners looked to him like land pirates; they probably hadn't done a day's honest work in their entire lives. They lived off of the land and the land's people that they could steal from or cheat out of. The cash he paid the store owner would have been enough scent to send them looking for that one person with any cash in his pockets. Most drifters were broke and living off credit until the next windfall. Slocum glanced over his shoulder and looked off down through the pine timber. He never doubted her observation; his only concern was how to lose them or settle their hash.

He motioned for her to ride ahead. She swung her horse around and took the lead rope from him. He busted the lagging bay good on the rump with his reins. Dang his sorry hide, he better learn to get up and go. The bay tucked his tail up the crack of his butt and jumped forward. His head high beside her, she set out past the lagging pack animal in a long trot and he kept close to her mount. The whipping might be enough to hold his attention, Slocum hoped, and glanced one more time down the mountain.

No sign of them—but he knew they were back there; Two Bird had spotted them and until he did something about them, they'd be there and up to some kind of mischief. He had his work cut out. His real desire was to cut through to Red Elk's sanctuary and find him. Those two only added to his problem. They might stumble onto Red Elk and in the process get Dorothy killed. No, he needed to deal with the buckskinners first, then find Red Elk.

They crossed the open country, pressing their animals until they reached some juniper brush at the base of the range. He slipped off his hard-breathing mount, handed her the reins and jerked the Winchester out of the scabbard.

"Hide back there," he said, meeting her coal-black gaze. She nodded in approval and booted her horse, taking the other two with her. Slocum knelt down, searching for signs of pursuit. They wouldn't be far behind. He wouldn't have much time to decide what to do about them. It was him and her or them as far as he could ascertain. He levered in a cartridge and tried to see across the sunlit brown grassland.

Two riders came into view. He squinted to make them out. Their hats did not look like the buckskinners' floppy head gear. Who were they?

"Who are they?" Two Bird asked, rejoining him.

"I ain't certain, but it isn't who I thought it was."

"One white woman?"

"Must be the woman from the trading post. Who's with her?"

"Young white man."

"Yeah, it's the blacksmith."

"Why they follow us?"

"Damned if I know, but it can't be good. Hold up!" he shouted to the two riders and came out from behind the boughs. "What are you two trailing us for?"

"Oh, thank God!" she gasped. "Billy and I had to get away. Can we go with you, mister?"

"We ain't going—" He shook his head, not wanting to tell her his business. But if she had those other three on their tail over her running away, he'd have more trouble.

"That's your husband."

"He don't treat me like I'm a wife."

"He's still your husband."

"Mister, he might be my paw, but he's mean and spiteful. He sure don't treat her like—well, a man should treat his wife."

"He's got lots of rights to come after you."

SLOCUM'S WARPATH   147

"So I can do his bidding?" she asked and used her hand to wipe the hair back from her face.

"Bidding, whatever—" Slocum tried to see if they had been followed.

"Even if he demanded that I sleep with one of those greasy hunters back there?" she asked, then swallowed hard.

"That's why we left," Billy said. Hardly dry behind the ears, he looked maybe eighteen.

Slocum shrugged. "We'll get you two out to the road to Espanola. I can't waste any more time than that."

"We'd sure be grateful," she said in relief.

"One thing, there's plenty of mad Apaches in the country between here and there. You two have any weapons?" They both shook their head. He closed his eyes. Ran off with only the clothes on their backs. What a fine situation. No supplies, not even a blanket, and they rushed away into the wilderness like God would take care of them.

"We better make camp. Two Bird." Then in Spanish, he told her to build a small fire.

"Can I help you?" Billy asked with the fresh look of youth ready to lend a hand.

"Unsaddle the horses and hobble them. I'm going to circle around and make sure they aren't coming in on us." Then he jerked up his right pant leg and drew out a .30-cap-and-ball Colt. He handed the handgun to him. "Don't use this unless you really have to."

"Yes, sir."

Slocum nodded and ran for his own horse. He wanted to make a wide circle to be certain those three weren't close by. With a lot to do before dark, he slammed the rifle in the boot and swung in the saddle. He left in hard lope. He knew that those three couldn't be more than an hour behind. Somehow he had to disable them and then move on with "his party." Two women and a strong-backed boy—it had to work. *Dorothy, oh, Dorothy, I'm coming.*

Close to sundown, he caught sight of three riders. The more familiar hats told him two were the buckskinners and the third had to be her man. They weren't on their earlier tracks, which made him wonder. Were they really after him and the errant wife or simply riding around? Damn, he wished he could read their minds. Then he decided they were headed for a small creek. Not a bad idea to water their animals; he planned to find water for his in the morning. Then he began to notice how drunk they were and could hear their hoots and raucous laughter.

Good, he would simply rest and let them make camp. Then he would slip in and take their animals. They couldn't go far drunk and on foot. It would save him having to kill them. He tethered his horse in the box elders and sat down. The sun would be set in an hour and he could rustle some horses.

Indian style, he began to move in on the camp. Their horses were ground tied and grazed through their bits. The three in camp were sitting close to the fire and Milt was passing the crock around. He could hear them talking in slurred voices.

"—Yeah, to a good piece of ass!"

"I-I promise you'll get some—when—we get her back."

"That boy of yours been dicking her?"

"Naw—he don't know nothing."

"Why she leave with him then?" Next came a belch that would have made a bullfrog blush and some laughter.

Slocum had the reins and led their horses quietly to the west away from the camp. Each step he made easy and took his time lest they heard him. The horses did not handle well and the gray wanted to kick the sorrel, but Slocum hissed him out of it. Then he went on until he was deep in a draw that led to the north and in rainy times fed the rushing creek. Mounted on the sorrel, the others in tow, he rode slowly, still being careful not to attract their attention.

At last, with his own horse added to the bunch, he headed for camp. A quarter-mile away, he heard the loud, distant squall that carried through the night.

"You hoss-stealing red bastards! I'll get you!"

A grin cracked his split lip. *Bet you will. I bet you will.*

At camp, he slipped down and the impressed-acting youth came in the starlight to take them. "Wow, you got their horses."

"And two Sharp's rifles too. We aren't so low on guns and ammo now."

"You have to kill them?"

"No." Slocum shook his head. "They were drunk, so I took

their horses. We better saddle the rest; I want to move on tonight. They might sober up."

"Who was with him?" Clare asked.

"Them two in buckskin," he said, taking a cup of coffee from Two Bird.

"Ugh," Clare said and her shoulders shuttered.

"Got beans and rice, you eat," Two Bird said in Spanish. "We get horses ready."

"*Si.*" He squatted down and blew the steam off the coffee. It would take three days to get them two close enough to Espanola to safely leave them. Then he and Two Bird could head for the sacred mountains. What a mess this whole six weeks had been. He'd ridden out of Colorado to shake a pair of bounty hunters on his heels, and since that day when he found Dorothy, it had been one wild goose chase after the other.

Somewhere out in the night, a coyote howled at the moon. He nodded thanks for the bowl of beans and rice she gave him and took the spoon. Slowlike he chewed on them. Somehow he had to get Dorothy away from Red Elk and to some doctor who could help her. Maybe in Sante Fe there would be one. Combs had left enough money. He shook his head, recalling the man wanting to kill her. May he rest in peace.

"I got them hosses ready, sir," Billy said.

"Be right there," Slocum said. He turned his attention back to the tasty dish. What would he do with all his wards? Maybe time would work things out for all of them. The coyote's mournful whooping filled the night. Slocum sure hoped so.

Chapter 22

By sunup, they had watered their animals at a moon lake, hobbled them and hidden out of sight in a small meadow. Clare thoroughly shook out the buckskinners' blankets before she allowed Billy to take one to wrap in against the chilly air.

"Might have anything in them," she said in disgust.

They soon were scattered on the ground in blankets and rolls. Slocum, satisfied there were no Indian signs about the area, covered his head and slept sound for a few hours. At noontime, he awoke, slipped out to relieve his bladder and see what was stirring around them.

He sighted some elk, cows and calves grazing to the southwest. Good, he decided, they were wary enough and they wouldn't be simply grazing if any bunch of bucks were around or the threesome. He vented his water and when he completed his task, he tried to think how far they dared go before dark. The way ahead could harbor war parties. To ride into one unsuspecting band would be suicidal for the four of them. To the east, the great gorge of the Rio Grande made a slice in the earth to rival the Grand Canyon. To the west was the mountain range where he would rather be than on this open tableland, but he needed to get a hundred miles south, send Clare and Billy on to a friendly pueblo or village, then head back and look for Red Elk and Dorothy.

He exhaled in a sharp breath. Apaches or not, they must

150

ride hard to the south. Use the extra horses in shifts and try to make some contacts with friendly people. In the midday sun, he could see the distant range of the medicine man's sacred place. *I'm coming, girl. Hold on.*

They ate some jerky, cinched up and rode. Two Bird took the lead and he told her to ride hard.

"You think there are Indians?" Clare asked, white-faced, as they charged southward.

"Always," he said and whipped the pack horse to make him go faster.

They rested long enough to relieve themselves. Slocum made sure Billy had one of the Sharp's on his horse as they switched to the fresh ones. Slocum kept his own pony to ride. The tough stud had lots of bottom.

"Have you seen any sign of them?" Clare asked, trying to mount the gray.

Slocum shook his head. "No sign yet. If we can ride like this, we may make it across here."

"Good," she said and licked her dry lips.

He wanted to tell her not to do that, but instead he reined his sweaty pony around and motioned for them to mount up and get going. There was no time to waste.

Two Bird took the lead, jerking on the lazy one. Billy rode in and sent the derelict off with a few quick lashes. Slocum gave him a shout of encouragement. He glanced back across the purple sage desert. No columns of dust. Good, they might make it to a safe haven, if the horses held up.

Saddle leather creaking in protest, horses' shoulders covered in lather, dripping wet and wheezing for breath, he finally halted them to a hard walk. Everyone gave a sigh, including the horses making snorts in the dust. They couldn't take much more.

"We can make the stage station at Abuda," Two Bird said.

"What?" Clare asked.

"We're going to head east and try to find the stage station at Abuda. Two Bird knows a way. It's on the Taos stage route along the river."

"Can she find it in the dark?" Clare asked.

"Better than I could," he said.

Two Bird smiled. He noticed it. She had heard the woman's English and understood it.

"Better ride before the horses stiffen," he said and Two Bird took the lead.

Long past midnight, the dogs began to set up a yapping party. Slocum saw lights being lit below as they came off the steep trail.

"Friend or foe?" a voice challenged them in Spanish.

"Amigos! Amigos!" he and Two Bird shouted.

"My God, where do you come from, hombre?" the armed guard asked.

"Pagosa awhile back," Slocum said and dropped heavily from the saddle.

"Damn, with women?" The man blinked in disbelief at his party as they dismounted like stiff tin soldiers.

"That wasn't by choice. Do you have some boys could walk our horses until they cool?"

"I would have to pay them?"

"No, I will pay them and well."

In Spanish, the man called to the lighted doorway. A woman appeared and looked them over, then she replied she would get them. Two Bird hung back, but a toss of his head made her come forward and join the others as they went inside. Soon, some young boys, sleepy eyed, came in the room and were instructed how to cool the horses. On the end, their father said, "You must do it right or the rich gringo will not pay you."

Two Bird chuckled over the last remark as she took a seat at the table where their hostess told them to sit. Soon plates of hot food and tortillas were served. Slocum could only wonder at the woman and her daughters' efficiency. But the rich, spicy food soon made him too tired to care.

The man, Raphael, asked Slocum small questions as he ate too much of the tasty dishes prepared by the stage stop keeper's wife, Nina. Everyone was so busy eating, they looked up in shock when Slocum raised his coffee cup.

"Let us toast these fine people and their wonderful food."

Clare blinked as if taken back, then she set down her fork and nodded in the affirmative. Billy's head bobbed in agreement as he hoisted his drink. Nina nodded in pride and smiled.

"Not often do you ever eat such fare at a roadhouse," Slocum said, going back to his eating.

"Yes," Raphael said. "You saw no Apaches?"

"No. We were lucky. Is the army out there?"

"A few companies. They need more troops."

"Have there been more raids down this way?"

"Only on the small ranches."

Slocum nodded. "Can those two catch the stage here?" He motioned to Clare and Billy.

"Sí."

"You have some money?" Slocum asked Clare.

"Yes." She frowned at him.

"Good, you can take the stage to Espanola. They won't dare bother you there."

"Yes," she said as if uncertain. "We'll go there next, Billy."

He agreed without even looking up from his eating.

"Raphael, they need to sell their horses. Do you buy such?"

"Certainly. The Apaches have raided so many, the market for ones to ride is good."

"There, that's settled," Slocum said and reached for another flour tortilla. He needed one more to wrap around the last of the meat and peppers on his plate.

"Will we see the two of you again?" Clare asked Slocum.

"Perhaps, we have business—"

"The woman that the Apaches took," she interrupted him. "Two Bird told me all about her."

"Dorothy Combs. I feel we need to try to recover her."

Clare made a displeased face at his words. "Isn't that the army's job?"

"Probably." Slocum said, considering the tortilla wrap in his fingers. "But they are busy after hostiles."

"I hope she appreciates your determination when you find her." Then she dropped her head and wearily shook it. "I am very grateful that you brought us here. I suspect in our ignorance we might have been killed or worse yet taken back."

"You're here now. That's behind you." He took a bite and savored the rich tastes of spices and the mesquite-smoked meat flavor. A man could sit at this table, eat her rich food, die there, then pass into heaven and never miss a step.

The young boys came in and announced shyly that the horses were cooled, watered and in the corral. Slocum paid each wide-eyed youth a dime a piece and they mumbled, *"Gracias."*

Then Raphael showed them to the bunk room. They brought in their blankets and climbed in, groaning about their fullness, and soon were asleep. Slocum shook himself awake in the predawn and went outside. He studied the rushing Rio Grande that swept past the stage stop on its long journey south to the Gulf. In the deep shadows of the craggy hills and under the fluttering cottonwoods, he considered what he must do next.

Find Dorothy. He ran the edge of his teeth over his sun-cracked lower lip. One more try. He needed to know she was safe, she didn't deserve any less. Clare could take her boy lover and go to Santa Fe and escape her husband's sorry ways. He turned at the soft sounds of her moccasins and considered Two Bird.

"Should I saddle our horses?" she asked.

"We both can," he said and grinned at her.

She hugged his waist as they headed for the corral. "You treat a squaw nice."

"Drag her over the mountains and back. That's nice?" he chuckled.

"No. Last night, you asked me in that place like I was white woman."

"Never considered anything else," he said.

She shook her head. "I know someday we will part, but I will never forget you."

He squeezed her thin shoulder. "Yes, someday I must ride on." He hadn't thought much about the bounty hunters on his back trail. They'd come: Ferd and Lyle Abbott, the two deputies out of Fort Scott, Kansas. He looked up the canyon at the towering peaks in the north. Like mountains, they'd always be back there.

Their horses were saddled and their packsaddle and panniers were on the gray. Slocum decided to let Clare and Billy have the slow bay to sell. Raphael came and put his arms on the corral.

"You will eat before you leave, amigo?"

"Wouldn't miss it," Slocum said and clapped his hands together to brush off the dirt and horse dander.

"You look for the woman they say has lost her mind?"

"Mrs. Combs, you know her?"

"I have heard of her. Her husband came through here frequently."

"He died. Must've had a stroke."

Raphael nodded.

"What did he do besides ranch?" Slocum led two of their ponies out and hitched them.

"I heard he was a big gambler."

"Makes sense," Slocum agreed.

"Will she lead you to her?" Raphael motioned to Two Bird bringing out the gray.

"She's a big help."

"I bet she is. Come and eat."

"We will."

Two Bird hitched the lead and pushed the ill-tempered gray over so he didn't kick at their horses. She looked after Raphael then turned her gaze to Slocum.

"What did he know?"

"Said Combs was a gambler."

She shrugged as they started for the station. "Perhaps the attack did not turn her to the spirits."

"You mean she was already like that?"

"I wonder."

"Guess we'll never know, will we? Let's eat and ride."

"Yes."

Slocum looked at the tops of the ridgeline as the first rays of the sun shone on the west wall of the canyon. Like a curtain being dropped, the golden sunlight began to dance on the black rock outcroppings. The cottonwoods rustled in the fresh wind and he wondered about her. *Dorothy, we're coming.*

Chapter 23

They rode westward seeing little tracks or sign of anything. They crossed the first range through a high pass and were in the next basin by sundown. Camped beside a stream, he used some green walnuts in a sack to stun enough cutthroat trout for their supper and breakfast.

She laughed from her place on the bank, busy gutting them. "I never ate them before. They always said they would make you sick."

He shook his head, pulling on his socks and boots after wading in the icy stream after the fish. "That's not true."

"They have not killed me so far," she said and bent over to flush the guts out the body cavity of another one.

"I have known men who would have paid a good price to come up here and fish for them."

"How do white men do that? With walnuts?"

"No." He laughed, stomping on his boots. "They use long sticks and hooks that look like insects on a long string."

She shrugged off the explanation, no doubt as something else strange for her to know about white men. Slocum stretched his arms over his head. In another day they should be close enough to learn if Red Elk was in his mountains. He gazed at the red sundown on the peaks and yawned. They'd made good miles. The hobbled horses grazed on the brown grass and the world around them appeared at peace.

They finished their meal of fish and crackers. She whipped

out their bedrolls in the dying twilight as he sat and smoked half of a small cigar. Then she stripped off her leggings, and took a seat before him. The flash of the small fire's flames danced on her shapely legs. He nodded in approval as she stood up and drew the fringed doeskin dress off over her head. He watched her shapely hips, the creases in her flat belly and the shake of her pear shaped breasts as she fought the garment off her head. At last with it on her arms, she smiled at him—the same way he figured Eve must have smiled at her mate when clothes became necessary to wear and she at last shed hers for him.

He toed off his boots, undid his shirt and removed his pants when he stood up to face her. She stepped in and began to undo the buttons on underwear. Her small hands rubbed over his skin and the corded muscles of his stomach. By the time he had shed his underwear, her hand cradled his scrotum, deftly balancing both balls like a juggler. Then she grasped his half-stiff rod and pulled on it as she pressed her rock-hard nipples to his lower belly. He hugged her tight and considered the pleasure ahead. His erection stiffened under her massaging and soon she pulled him down on the bedroll.

He came between her raised knees and she guided him into the gates of pleasure. Her soles threaded on the backs of his knees as she arched her back to accept him. The tight sleeve began to squeeze him and the contractions grew stronger. They hunched faster, caught up in the whirlpool of maddening desire. She pulled him down on her. Soon their pubic bones ground like great millstones atop each other. Her needlelike wick rubbing the top of his shaft with each thrust in and out.

Breath became a short commodity. Her legs locked around him and she pumped her butt to meet his every move in her. Then his fierce erection reached the bursting point and he felt the draw from deep in his sack. Like hot arrows in his butt, the force rising up his stem soon threatened to split apart the head of his dick. She cried out loud and he drove it home. The blast equaled the force of hydraulic gold mining inside her.

She grasped him tight, then fainted into a limb form under him. He shook his head to try and clear it. At last, they managed to crawl under the covers with her small body nested in his. Slocum raised up and listened to the night sounds. Nothing out of place, so he dropped back down, cuddled around her small form and cupped one breast in his fingers and fell asleep.

In the predawn, he caught the horses and they began saddling. She turned an ear and frowned. He stopped with the saddle in his hands.

"What is it?"

"I heard a horse."

"Which way?" He looked at their animals. Horses knew things before men did. The gray had his ears pitched to the north and was looking for something. Slocum tossed his pack on his horse. He tried to see what interested the animal, then he caught the gray by the muzzle to silence him. He could see horses and travois. It was a party on the move, with the jingle of tin bells and voices of children. He took their horses behind a screen of junipers. She came behind him.

"You know them?"

"Yes, they are from Sitting Horse's camp."

"They warlike or friendly?"

She shrugged. "My sister is among them."

"Where they headed?"

"I don't know."

"Best we stay hid?"

She nodded.

Then a buck rode around the junipers. He reined up and Slocum's hand shot for his Colt. For a long moment, they stared at each other. Then Two Bird spoke in Apache at him.

"He is my cousin, Black Deer," she said, standing between Slocum and the Apache who was fighting with his stomping horse.

"Good. Tell him we're friends."

She spoke again to the brave who had shed his blanket in the struggle to contain his horse. But her words did not change the anger written on his copper face.

His words back to her were harsh and he motioned to Slocum.

She spoke again as the pony danced about in a circle, making the brave vulnerable and even more upset with his unruly mount. He used both hands to jerk on the jaw bridle, but his cold stare was upon Slocum when he wasn't fighting his pony.

"I told him you only seek the white woman," she said over her shoulder, still keeping herself in front of him like a shield.

Slocum nodded, his hand on his gun butt. Black Deer could decide. A broad-chested warrior in his late twenties, his bangs were cut short and he wore a small red skull cap. His chest was covered by a porcupine-quilled vest. It was the streaks of black paint on his high cheeks that emphasized his manner. He looked warlike enough and equally shocked that a white man dared invade his land.

"Tell him we go in peace to find her."

She shook her head. "He wants to die."

"Then let's get it over with."

"No. He must kill me first. You are my guest."

"I'm not for that." Slocum considered the redwood handles on the Colt in his sweaty grasp.

"He won't kill me. I am his kin."

"I ain't so certain of that." The look on that Apache's face was one of outright anger.

She held up her hand to stop Slocum. "I can handle him."

Her words in Apache were sharp and the buck leaped from his horse, but it caused the pony to fly back and he soon was forced to hold on with both hands as it shied backward. Tossing and shaking its head, its butt crashed into the junipers and the paint felt back on his haunches. He rose trembling as the buck charged in and began to kick it in the sides with his pointed-toe moccasins.

Soon laughter began to ring out. A gray-haired Indian rode up laughing hard at the upset buck. He nodded to Slocum at last and then a half dozen more rode into the glade. The scowling buck led the paint out from the bushes and shook his head in disapproval at their amusement.

"Sitting Horse," she said, indicating the chief.

Slocum felt their stares were on him and her. The odds went up. Way up. First he had one mad Indian, now he had the tribe. Then a squaw, holding up her leather dress so she could run, came through the juniper as excited as a child, screaming something like a name.

Two Bird shrieked and ran to hug her. Obviously the sister or someone she knew well.

"Sitting Horse," the old man announced.

"Slocum."

Sitting Horse nodded as if that was nice. "You come. We smoke. Find food." He shook his head at the two woman crying and slapping each other. "They can bring your horses."

Then he dropped off his short, coupled horse. Bowlegged and showing some stiffness, he fell in beside Slocum. He glanced back, but Two Bird was chattering at a million words a minute to the other woman.

"You know the white chief?"

"At Fort Union?" Slocum asked.

"Yes."

"No, but why do you need to know him?"

"If we could talk to him—"

"About no food and tough beef."

Sitting Horse nodded. Then a taller Indian strode up beside him on the right and spoke in Spanish. "There is no game. The cows that they bring us to eat are already jerky on the hoof."

"That is Tall Man," the chief said as he pointed ahead to where the women and children were gathered. They looked at Slocum with saucer eyes and awe.

"I would go there and speak for you, if you would deliver to me the crazy white woman that Red Elk keeps in his camp."

Tall Man tore into a rampage in Apache. Obviously he did not like the deal Slocum offered. While Slocum glanced back over his shoulder wishing for his translator, Two Bird and several women led his outfit. Too far away to be much good to him, he turned back, trying to figure out how much power of a horse trade he had with these men.

They wanted to quit the warpath. Surely the officer in charge would listen and get something done on their behalf. Buying Indians good beef was a lot cheaper than sending out soldiers. Still, Slocum knew from the past how corrupt the Indian Bureau was. Their agents were the worst government agents in existence for their graft, bribery and corruption.

Sitting Horse showed him a place on a buffalo hide. With

a nod, Slocum took his seat, and the other soon joined him on blankets and skins in a circle. Apparently this was the chief's own place, for no others sat upon it but him and the leader.

Women rushed about; one brought him a bowl of water to drink.

"No whiskey," Sitting Horse said as if to apologize.

Slocum shrugged as if it was unimportant. He sipped on the cool liquid and nodded his approval.

"If we can bring this woman to you? When could you go to the white chief?"

"Very quickly." He glanced over at the man.

"Good." Sitting Horse rose and brushed off his butt as he waddled over to two young men. They nodded to the chief's words and then took off on a run.

The older man returned. "She will be here by dark." He sat down again and gave some orders to one of the women. She nodded and was gone.

Two Bird came over, knelt behind him and whispered in his ear. "Sitting Horse has sent for the woman. You know that?"

Slocum nodded.

"Red Elk will be very angry when he comes."

"Who is the boss?"

She glanced around, then cupped her hands over his ear. "This council."

"What can I do to help it?"

"They wish for you to speak peace for them. They are afraid the army will shoot first if they find them. Many women and children would be killed."

"I savvy."

The women served them berries in honey. The others ate with their fingers and licked them clean. Two Bird brought him a spoon. He nodded in approval at the sweet mixture and licked his lips realizing the treat of the dessert that they served him.

"Will the white chief listen?" Sitting Horse asked.

"I am certain he will. He wants no more war with the Apaches."

"Good, but we will need food."

"I will have him send food."

Sitting Horse acted satisfied at those words and sat back to finger-eat his treat.

The sun set behind the mountains and they had fresh elk meat, broiled on fire. Ribs were served him by Two Bird and some flour tortillas. They were as fresh as the meat and melted in his mouth. She sat behind him, telling him about things she had learned.

The band had been busy dodging army patrols. They had only left the reservation to find food, but that made them on the warpath and hostiles as far as the agency was concerned.

Then several horses came at a gallop, and on tall sorrel paint, Red Elk charged into the camp with the gleaming blade of his lance reflecting in the council's firelight. He leaped from the horse and stalked over with the lance ready. Sitting Horse grunted and bolted to his feet swifter than Slocum expected.

In a furious exchange between the two men, the chief finally took away his lance and tossed it aside. Then they had a chin to chin argument until finally Red Elk sat down and folded his arms in defiance.

With a wry set to his large mouth, Sitting Horse came back and took his place.

"You are not her man!" Red Elk shouted.

"She belongs with her own people," Slocum said, amazed at the Apache's English.

"She lives with spirits."

Slocum agreed.

"What do you have to trade me?" Red Elk demanded.

"Horses, guns, money?"

"No, I want a woman."

Slocum felt his eyebrows frown and his eyes narrow at the man's impossible demand. What the hell did he think—horses he could buy. They were the wealth of the Apache. But a woman . . .

He felt Two Bird's small hand on his shoulder. "Tell him I will be his woman."

Slocum shook his head. No way that he would agree to that.

"It would be an honor to be such a shaman's wife."

"His slave?" he whispered back at her.

"Yes." The words sent a cold shiver up his spine. She was serious.

"I want to see the white woman," Slocum said and looked to Sitting Horse who agreed with a nod. Red Elk rose and waved. The two boys guided Dorothy to the firelight.

The look on her face knifed him. She needed a bath, her clothes were in rags but she had that innocent air about her like she was no part of this whole affair. They eased her down and when seated she began rocking from side to side as if she had her own music.

Slocum dropped back and nodded. "You sure, girl?"

"Don't worry for me. Should I step out there?"

"It is your decision. I won't ask you to do it."

She used his shoulder to rise up and go by him. It caused a hush to fall on the camp. Only the snap of the fire and a few dogs growling over the possession of bones.

"I will be the trade," she said in Spanish.

Red Elk looked for a long time at her. Slocum could barely see him except though the space she made between her legs.

"You are the whore of a white man," Red Elk scoffed in Spanish.

"What has she been?" Two Bird indicated Dorothy. "Can you not make love to a real woman?"

Red Elk's face looked ready to explode. To be so openly challenged in the face of the other men in the tribe was a flagrant slap upon his manhood. Then he grinned.

"He about killed me once, only his powder was bad. Now he gives me his castoff."

"She goes by her own choice," Slocum said, loud enough so the man could hear him.

Red Elk stopped and looked hard across the circle. Then he rose, came across the circle and took her by the arm.

"The spirits have her. You never will," he said in Spanish to him and led Two Bird by the arm across the circle.

"Take the pack horse and yours," Slocum said after her.

She never nodded, never looked back. Obediently, she followed Red Elk into the shadows and soon the night resounded with the drum of retreating hooves.

He stared across the campfire and his ward sat swaying from side to side. Lord, what had he done? Get her to a doctor, to some help. The enormity of his situation threatened to overwhelm him.

"Now there will be peace," Sitting Horse announced with finality.

God. I hope so.

Chapter 24

Slocum dropped off the hillside toward Tatum's trading post, which sparkled in the dancing sunlight under the cottonwoods. Dorothy hummed a child's song on the paint horse that she rode and he led. Not once did she call him by any name; she went along and did what he told her to do in an abstract way.

"You found her," the younger woman, Jill, shouted and rushed out. Then with her mouth open, she stopped and gazed in dismay at Dorothy.

Slocum stepped down, hitched his horse. "She isn't exactly herself," he explained as the woman clapped both hands over her mouth.

"She needs a bath and some clothes."

Numb-like, Jill nodded, still frozen in her tracks.

"She won't hurt you. She's very congenial."

"Oh, yes," she managed with an exhale.

"What's wrong, Slocum?" Sid asked, coming out on the porch.

"Dorothy Combs ain't in great shape."

"Got her mind, didn't it?"

Slocum nodded and undid his cinches. "Load me up two hundred pounds of corn meal and fifty pounds brown sugar on this pack horse."

"What you doing with that?"

"Giving it to that boy sitting on that paint horse up there."
He indicated the top of the ridge to the west.

"Why, he's an Apache."

"Yeah," Slocum said. "Toss in ten pounds of coffee and
a big sack of hard candy."

"Who's buying it?"

"A dead man." Slocum nodded. "A dead man."

Sid shrugged and went inside. Slocum began unloading
his things out of the panniers.

The two Tatum women guided Dorothy inside the house.
The oldest shook her head privately at Slocum. He agreed.
Perhaps there was no helping the woman, but he sure hoped
there would be somewhere he could find some. He turned
back to his chore of readying the panniers.

The items were soon loaded in them and on foot, Slocum
led the gray around the corral. He made a big arm wave at
the youth, who came bounding down the hillside on his paint.

"Here is some food until I can get the white father to send
more," he said to the boy.

The youth agreed with a solid nod and took the lead. Then,
with a yip, his paint and the gray were cat-hopping up the
hillside.

"You trade her for that food?" Sid asked, coming beside
him.

Slocum shook his head. No, he gave a lot more than that
for her. The reflection made him wonder about Two Bird and
how she was making it in Red Elk's camp. He hoped she
was all right; somehow he knew she would survive, but he
felt guilty letting her do that for him.

The women gave Dorothy a bath and dressed her in fresh
clothing to replace her filthy rags. They combed and brushed
her hair, which hung in dark curls again. They sat her in the
rocker on the front porch and when Slocum came around the
corner from his own bath and shave in the shed out back, he
stopped in his tracks.

Butterflies flittered around her. Colorful ones, ones to
match her dark hair and others flew around her like they
swarmed a patch of flowers in the desert. Did they know
something about her? He shook his head and let the fresh
smell of shaved soap run up his nose. If she realized his
presence, she gave no notion as she hummed away.

He climbed the porch and stopped to stare across the broad basin. They needed to get on their way. Maybe he could find a rig in Espanola to drive them to Fort Union.

"Ruff," she said in a soft voice. "I'm ready to go on, aren't you?"

"Yes, Dorothy. I sure am."

He looked over at her, frowned and then when he got no response, he went inside the trading post.

"Thanks, Jill. She looks very nice."

"She talks funny."

"What's that?" he asked, taking a cigar from the tin humidor. "Put it on my bill."

"Fine. She talks about going to dances."

"Probably when she was younger."

"Maybe." Jill shook her head. Then in low voice she said, "She's a whole lot worse than she was before, isn't she?"

Slocum agreed. "When I first found her she was upset. Now she's worse."

"In the hands of that Indian—" Jill shook her head, looking afraid and upset. "It must have been terrible."

Slocum agreed and went back out to smoke. No one would ever know about her days with Red Elk unless she opened up. Perhaps no one needed to know about any of it. He sat on the stoop. Cut off the end with a jack knife and licked the entire length of the tube to slow the burn. He intended to enjoy the entire cigar and not be interrupted.

He struck a match on the adze-shaped flooring and drew deep. Somewhere out there he needed to find the army. The Tatums had not seen them since the raid. In reality, he hoped they were around Espanola—then he could give them the word about the Apaches' wish to surrender and ride on to Santa Fe to find someone to take care of Dorothy. He drew on the cigar and let the smoke fill his lungs, then slowly exhaled.

The nicotine soon began to settle him. In Santa Fe, he would write Jim Bob Phillips and let him figure out what needed to be done about her. Perhaps in Fort Worth or Dallas there was a specialist who handled such things. He had no idea. Another deep drag on his cigar and she began to creak the porch boards.

"Good to be back, Ruff," she said.

"Yes, Dorothy. It is."

He wondered about her. Was her mind coming back? No way to know. She was humming again and making the rocker's runners creak on the porch flooring.

They left Tatum's in the predawn. She rode the gentle sorrel, and his was a blood bay. Both animals were fresh; they left in good jogging trot. The concerned Tatum women had worried about how he would care for her. He assured them he could handle things and that they would be in Espanola in two days. If Dorothy knew anything—he couldn't be certain. She numb-like agreed to be led and obeyed him.

Her whole being left him empty. A hollowness that went unfilled. Nothing he did or said changed her bland ways. He saw no light in her eyes. She was in some land of her own and not to be disturbed by earthly happenings around her. When he glanced back from time to time, her look showed no signs of recognition.

At noontime, they watered the animals at a small stream. She went off to relieve herself and returned about the time he had begun to wonder if sending her off by herself was such a good idea.

He helped her on the sorrel and as she swung her leg over, she smiled.

"At last, we don't have to worry about him, do we?"

"No, we don't have to worry about him," he said to reassure her, but felt guarded. Who did she mean? Her husband? Red Elk?

"I haven't dreamed about that savage for several nights now," she said as if that bothered her. "You know he use to come to me in my dreams?"

"Yes," Slocum said and mounted his own horse.

She swept the hair from her face. "I dreamed of another man with whiskers." A shake of her head as if she wished to clear it. "Why did they all rape me?"

"Good question," he said. Without an answer to satisfy her, he groped in his mind for one.

"Ruff, why do you stay with me? I've been violated by so many."

"I want to help you."

"Help me?"

He turned and saw she had begun to cry. Her shoulders shook with sobs; streams of tears rushed down her face. Was she breaking down? He couldn't see her eyes for her fists that were socked into them. Filled with anxiety, he reined in his horse and jumped down. Half stumbling in the loose sand to get to her, he swept her off the sorrel and carried her in his arms to the shade of a small cottonwood.

There he knelt and set her down. Moving the strands of hair away from her face, he held her head in his lap. Her flooded hazel eyes met his and he knew that she was there. There for the first time since he found her at the burning cabin.

"I've been far away—haven't I?"

"Yes."

She started to struggle to rise then settled back on his arm and legs. "My husband—"

"He's dead. He had a stroke."

Her mouth opened, her gaze grew stronger. "When?"

"A week, two weeks ago."

"The funeral?"

"He had one."

She closed her wet lashes and drew in a shuddering breath. "I wasn't even there for it?"

"He was searching for you."

"That was a dream, wasn't it? I thought it was."

He nodded, hoping her talking about it was bringing some form of closure.

"Ruff's dead too?"

"Yes." That proved she was herself, she knew he wasn't the cowboy.

"Where are we?" She sat up and rubbed her eyes to clear them.

"On our way to Espanola."

"What will we do there?"

He rose and pulled her to her feet. "Find the army and tell them the Apaches want peace."

"I can ride my own horse now."

"I think that you can."

"Do me a big favor."

"What's that."

"Hold-me-until this-trembling-stops—"

He reached out and drew her close to him. The tremors in her body came in waves. She clutched him hard, but they kept on. At last, with her making shivering sounds despite the warm sun, the chills stopped. With a frown, he looked into her pale white face.

She swallowed and managed, "I'll be fine now."

"We can wait a little while."

"No, we better go find the army."

He helped on the sorrel and tied up the lead rope, giving her the reins.

"I don't even know your name?"

"Slocum."

"I'll repay you, Slocum. Somehow, someday." She nodded and turned the sorrel, ready to ride.

He swung in the saddle and gave an exhale of relief. Go find the army. *Dorothy, oh, Dorothy, you've made my day.*

Chapter 25

"Don't move a muscle, squaw man." The sulfurous muzzle of a Colt was in his face. Slocum sat up in the starlight, braced on his arms behind him.

"Where in the hell's my wife, you sumbitch?" someone else broke in.

"That ain't her over there?" the gun toter asked.

"Hell, no."

Slocum's heart sunk. It was Milt Ricketts and those two buckskinners, what ever their names were. How? Why? He needed to figure a way out of this and fast.

"I ain't got your wife. What the hell is wrong with you?" Slocum growled.

"Listen, tough guy," the buckskinner jammed the pistol hard in his face. "We're asking the damn questions, not you."

"Burt?"

"Yeah, Snively?" the gunman said to his partner.

Good, there was Ricketts, Burt and Snively, the unbathed pirates from Colorado. In the bottom of the bedroll was the .30 caliber Colt. The one he carried in his boot all the time. Thank God, he had gotten it back from Billy when he gave the boy the Sharp's. But he might get Dorothy shot in the melee that it caused when he went for it.

"This lady says her name is Combs."

"Aw, hell, who cares. Ask her what Slocum did with my wife?" Ricketts said.

"She don't know."

All Slocum could think about how did these bandits manage to sneak in his camp and jump him. With Dorothy in her fragile mental condition, she didn't need more trial by these three worthless ticks.

"Get up and get dressed," Burt ordered and he stood up.

The opportunity was right. He lifted his boot, poured it out as was his habit so no lurking critter like a scorpion or vinegaroon was in it when he put his foot into it. Then partially under the covers he drew on the left one. Burt acted interested in those two talking to her. In that brief moment as if struggling to pull it on, he slid the small revolver in his vamp. Then he put on the second one.

Burt swept up his holster and knife, then he herded Slocum over to where Dorothy and the others were standing.

"What we going to do with them?" Burt asked.

"What the hell did you do with my wife?"

"I never had your wife."

"You're lying!" Ricketts screeched in his face.

"Well, she damn sure ain't here. You know about his wife and boy?" Burt asked Dorothy.

She shook her head.

"Listen, Ricketts," Snivelly began. "They ain't here, ain't no sign of them here. We can either kill these two or take their horses and go on."

"But damn, he had her."

"He don't now."

"What did you do with her?" Ricketts wheeled back and faced Slocum.

"I never had her."

"Damn funny that she left right after you did."

"She must have gone somewhere else." He tried in the first light to see how Dorothy was fairing through all of this.

"Get their horses," Burt ordered.

Slocum didn't like the way that the strong-smelling buckskinner was eying Dorothy. He might not leave her.

"You know who she is, don't you?" Slocum said.

"Who?"

"Wife of the chief U.S. marshal in Santa Fe. She's Milton Combs' wife. You touch her and you won't get anywhere."

Chances that Burt knew the man in charge were slim, so he hoped his bluff worked.

"Yeah, well I ain't afraid of no marshal."

"You will when they all get on your trail."

Snivelly came back with Ricketts leading all the horses. "We taking her for our pleasure?"

"Hell, no she's some law official's wife," Burt said and spit to the side. "Let's get the hell out of here." He mounted his horse and they fled into the peachy light cresting the range to the east.

"What did they mean—wife?" she asked, rushing over and hugging him.

"All a big lie, girl. I told them that to get rid of them."

"They took our horses?" She nestled her face in his shirt.

"We can walk a ways. It's better than their alternatives." He looked across the sagebrush and brown grass plains. Much better than their plans for the two of them.

"I was so afraid." She trembled under his arms.

"More border scum. It's over. We better get hiking." Someday, he would even that score with those three.

Midday, an Indian couple in a wagon gave them a bumpy ride in a wagon bed. They arrived in Espanola at dark. He found the army's camp and walked up to the main tent.

"Your business, sir?" an armed guard asked.

"Need to speak to the commander."

"Regarding?"

"Sitting Horse and several of the Apaches that wish to surrender."

"Yes, sir. Captain Crawley, man out here wishes to speak to you."

"Who?" The familiar figure, bareheaded, stood in the lamplight of the tent's interior.

"Slocum. Who's with you?"

"Mrs. Combs."

"Come in. Sorry, ma'am. Have you two eaten? Where are your horses?"

"We caught a ride with an Indian couple. Some outlaws stole our horses earlier."

"Private?"

"Yes, sir."

"Find some food and coffee for our guests."

"Yes, sir."

"Now tell me about Sitting Horse and his wanting to sur-render. Here take a chair." He showed them to the canvas folding ones around his desk.

"I was in his camp five days ago," Slocum began. "He wants some food for his people. He speaks of jerky on the hoof at the agency."

Crawley nodded. "We all suspected this."

"They're on the move so your soldiers don't swoop down on them and kill their women and children."

"Could you and a party go find the ones that want peace?"

"Yes, if you will see to Mrs. Combs' welfare."

Crawley nodded to her. "Of course. Sorry, ma'am, we have been so busy talking about Indians—"

"That's fine, I'm so grateful to be off that bumpy wagon, nothing is too much now." She smiled at him.

Everyone smiled.

"Who stole your horses?"

"Some rowdies named Snively, Burt and Ricketts."

"Why did they do that?"

"They burst into our camp early this morning . . ." Slocum told him the rest of the story about Ricketts wanting his wife back.

"You think they're in town. Here?"

"They could be."

"I'll have Sheriff Mendoza look for them."

"Fine, I'd like my horses back."

"Yes. Mrs. Combs, your food should be here shortly. Is there anything I can get you?"

"No, Captain. I am perfectly fine, thank you, sir."

Crawley nodded as if he believed her, her obvious beauty no doubt setting in on the man. Dorothy wasn't hard to look at, even a little disheveled from the wagon ride.

The food with a mess sergeant bearing a pot of coffee soon arrived and the noncom fussed over her. His Irish brogue rang clear in the night and he was a great flirt no doubt as well.

"Well, ma'am, the likes of you this man's army ain't seen."

"Thank you, sergeant."

"Sergeant O'Rourke. Ma'am, at your service. Now if that

meat's too tough for your knife, I carry a good sharp one on me."

"I imagine you do," she said and smiled at him.

That only set off his Irish ways and he fussed more over her. Crawley drank coffee and Slocum enjoyed the beef stew, which he scored above average for military fare.

Quarters for the lady were made up and she was excused: Slocum was to share Crawley's tent after the officers met and planned the scouting party to find the "friendlies."

So in the predawn light, he and Dorothy walked along the rushing Rio Grande.

"Will you wire your father?" he asked.

"I best do that," she agreed.

"I can't say when I will return." Slocum turned to her. "You have money."

"I do?"

"Yes, you husband left a sum with me." He dug out the money and pressed it in her hand. "Is there more in a bank?"

"Perhaps in Santa Fe. He did business there."

Slocum agreed. Did she know about his gambling?

"I wonder if his other wife knew?" she asked.

"Knew what?" He frowned at her.

"He—had another wife—children also, in Santa Fe."

"How long have you known that?"

"Two years," she said blandly. "Why I planned to leave him."

Slocum nodded. "What will you do now?"

"Go home to Texas, I guess."

"I need to see about the fresh horse they have for me."

"I understand." She posed her mouth for him and he kissed her. Then with dread he stepped back.

"Good luck, Dorothy."

"Oh, I will. You be careful." She fought back her obvious upset. "I never would have been here but for you."

He hugged her, finding it hard to swallow. "Sorry, but we must part."

"Can I pay you?"

He looked into her sad eyes. "No. Good luck."

She stood on her toes and kissed him. He forced himself to turn to away and hurried off to find his mount.

By dawn, the small company of a dozen troopers, including one Master Sergeant Hickel, two scouts and a young lieutenant named Davies, left Espanola with Slocum. Crawley gave Davies the order to follow Slocum's lead and try to bring in as many "friendlies" as they could. He sent messengers out to tell the troops in the field to back off until the peace process was completed.

By day two they were at Tatum's outpost.

"Oh, Slocum." Jill rushed out, hardly aware of the others. "How is poor Mrs. Combs?"

Slocum swept off his hat and wiped his sweaty face on his sleeve. "Actually quite well. She's planning to return to Texas. She knew who I was and everything at our parting."

Jill frowned. "But—"

"I don't know what happened. She came back to herself is all I know."

"Oh, how sorry—" She looked around at the rest of his party and as if flustered, rushed back inside the store.

"She was the lady who the Apaches took captive?" Davies asked.

Slocum nodded.

No sign of the Apaches around Tatum's. They had seen nothing.

"What shall we do next?" Davies asked.

"I want a half-day's head start tomorrow. I'm going to carry a good-size white flag and ride north. They see it and me, they might come in. Make no show of force, simply ride up my back trail."

"That could be dangerous."

Slocum agreed. "But if Sitting Horse wants peace, he'll contact us."

Davies didn't look or act convinced. "Captain said for you to take the lead. But that plan sure sounds risky."

"Guess we'll know by sundown tomorrow."

"Yeah, but it's spooky to me."

"Have a good white flag made and ready. I ride out at dawn."

The lieutenant shook his head. "I hope they don't want your scalp, sir."

Leading a pack horse loaded down with more corn, brown sugar and hard candy, Slocum rode out of Tatum's before first light. He headed across the great sagebrush flats and when the dawn peeked up, he studied the far-off San Juans in Colorado. No clouds—it would be a warm day.

At Mid-morning he saw them from the corner of his eye as they emerged from a dry wash: a woman, three children, two cur dogs, a horse and a travois.

"Ho!" she shouted and he nodded.

Over the next rise, they came off the far hillside, more women leading horses, more children, dogs and a few loose colts shaking their heads and dancing on their toes. He waved and shared, "Ho"s with them.

Somewhere ahead was line of cottonwoods. There would be a stream there. They could cook the corn meal and brown sugar, suck on his hard candy and wait for the army.

The party grew in numbers with each mile. Soon men began to appear. Wrapped in blankets they rode their ponies in to join the widely spread-out band.

At the stream, Slocum dismounted. He forced his heavy stick into the sand so the white flag could wave. Then he dug in the packs for the candy. He soon had to give a squaw a sack to pass them out to all the children who came around for some.

"I'd have never believed it," the lieutenant said, when he rode up. Looking over the swirling cooking fires, the Apaches nodded to him and his men. He bound off his horse and gave the reins to his noncom.

"Come, I want you to meet Sitting Horse," Slocum said and tousled a young Indian boy's hair. The youth looked up, his mouth bulging with candy, and grinned, showing his missing front teeth.

When Slocum returned to Espanola, he learned that Mrs. Combs had already caught a stage for Sante Fe. He sold his mount and took the same mode of transportation. He arrived after dark, shouldered his saddle and started for a hotel off the square.

"Slocum?" a woman's voice called out softly.

He stopped and turned to see Clare.

"Evening, ma'am." He tipped his hat to her. "Nice to see you."

"You need to get off the street," she said between her teeth.

"Why—"

"Don't ask questions." She steered him into a dark alleyway and looked back to be certain they were unheeded.

"What is it?"

"There's two men here asking about you. Name's Abbott."

"Thanks, guess I owe you—"

"You sure do—" With that she threw her arms around him and kissed him. Her efforts forced him to the adobe wall and he about dropped his saddle on her.

"What about Billy?" he asked between her hot kisses.

"Oh, he's fine."

"Good. If that's the Abbotts, I better—"

"Come along with me."

"Where're we going?"

"My place. Where they would never look for you."

Slocum looked at the stars he could see shining between the two buildings for celestial intervention. None immediately came. She tugged on his arm for him to go with her.

Two days later, he left Sante Fe in the early morning riding on top of a wagon load of cured cowhides. The sun was shining through the yellow canvas top and bathing him in the sunlight's filtered warmth while the sluggish oxen lumbered south. Benito's destination with the skins was a leather tannery yard at Coralilles. Slocum napped and thought about Clare and her hospitality; she had proved as interesting-looking undressed as she had been dressed.

At midday, they reached a campground for the afternoon along the river. Slocum helped him water the ox and make a fire to cook beans. The bovines were let loose to graze, and they went to take siestas by the wagon.

"Hey!" someone shouted.

Slocum raised the straw sombrero and peeked at the big man on the black-and-white Appaloosa horse.

"We're looking for a guy called Slocum."

"No savvy," he said and let the sombrero down.

"Damn dumb Messikins," Abbott swore. "Come on, Ferd, they don't know nothing."

The drum of their horses' hooves soon faded.

"Who did they want?" Benito asked sleepily.

"Some gringo named Slocum."

"Crazy, huh?"

"Yeah, loco."

Five days later, he helped Benito unload the hides at the tannery. Afterwards, they went to a cantina, ate a large meal and drank tequila. Slocum recognized the man when he came in the door, and he went to the bar. With his back toward him and in the clothes of a Mexican, he doubted the man would recognize him. Pappy had a drink at the bar, then asked the bartender about *putas*.

The bartender sent the man down the street and Slocum relaxed when he left. He parted with Benito the next morning, shook his hand and refused the money the man offered to pay him for his work.

At the livery, he was looking over the horses for sale when three men rode up. They were easy to recognize. It was Ricketts, Burt and Snivelly. Under the wide-brimmed sombrero, he wondered if they would recognize him.

They spoke quickly to the stable hand. The owner went forward, excusing himself from Slocum who remained in the pen, to see what they wanted.

He returned and the three drifted down the street. "They asked about a man called Slocum."

"You know him?" Slocum asked.

"No, I never heard of him," the man said, climbing on the fence and pointing to a bald-faced sorrel. "He's a good one. Funny thing, some gringos were here a few days ago asking for the same hombre."

"What for?"

"How should I know. You want the sorrel?"

"I want to try him."

"He is sound. You will like him."

Slocum tried to see where the threesome had gone in the cantina. Obviously they had not found Clare in Sante Fe, or why would they be looking for him? He hadn't seen those three since they stole his horses.

The saddle blanket in place on his new purchase, he tossed his hull on the sorrel, then cinched it down tight. The bald-faced pony acted a little snorty, but a horse worth his salt had some of that in him. He cheeked the bridle up close to his leg when he swung on. It forced the horse to circle, but restrained him from bucking.

Loud pops of bullets rang out down the street. It made the pony excited and he stuck his head down and began to buck. Slocum grabbed for his hat and away they went down the main street, the pony landing on his front feet and kicking over his back on the other end. With a fistful of reins, he tried to drag his head up but it did no good. The horse soon bucked past several house and finally Slocum managed to turn him back.

"Oh, I am so sorry—" the stableman apologized.

"That's all right. What's the bottom dollar?"

"Twenty dollars?"

"Sold." Slocum rose in the stirrups and dug up a double eagle. The man caught it on the fly. He waved and Slocum left Coralilles in a dead run.

Four days later, he was playing cards in the Red Slipper in Magdellena, New Mexico. His luck was holding good at cards. While several were taking a piss break, he looked up and saw a boy selling newspapers in the saloon.

"Bring me one," he said.

"Sure, mister. Be ten cents."

Slocum paid him and opened the front back. Three strangers had a shootout in Coralilles Saloon. Dead were Milt Ricketts and Adolph Snively, and taken to Dr. Green's, Burt Larson, who also died later of bullet-inflicted wounds. The three men came to town together and apparently got into a strong argument. Who shot who was being asked by the coroner, Louis Sanchez. Sanchez thought that they were alone in the altercation.

He turned over and read the next article. Apache Agent arrested. Sam Newsome, the current agent, faced federal charges of corruption in a warrant served today by Chief Marshal Tom Watts from Albuquerque. The Jicarilla Apaches of northern New Mexico territory will have a new agent as soon as the department can find one. Currently the agency is being managed by the U.S. Army. According to sources, all warlike activity by the tribe has ceased.

Mrs. Dorothy Combs, a recent widower, visited the city this week. She was clearing up the estate of her deceased husband, Milton Combs. Mrs. Combs has enlisted the services of the law firm of Snyder and Goins, a very well-respected organization in the territory's court system. Mrs. Combs planned to return to her state of origin, Texas, when all the matters of the estate have been settled.

"You ready to play?"

Slocum put down the paper and looked at the other players. "Oh, yes."

"Anything of interest in that paper?" the dealer asked.

"Not much," Slocum said. He took a sip of the whiskey and considered things. Gathering up his hand, he studied the cards. Take a week or so to ride that far. If she happened to be tired of Red Elk—he discarded two cards—where would Two Bird be at? With Sitting Horse's band, if she wasn't with that medicine man. Wouldn't take long to find out if she was free.

Then what would he do? Raise ten dollars. He had a full house, queens and aces. No, he might better go check on her. Call? Sure, he laid out the full house on the felt tabletop, then looked over their glum frowns.

"Gents, I need to be excused."

"Where're you going?"

"To go see about a berry picker."

"A berry picker?"

"Yeah, I think I know where one is. And gents thanks for the interesting evening." He tipped his hat to them, then filled it with his winnings.

Ten days later, he pushed the bay horse off the mountainside. With two pack mules on his heels, he dropped off of the pass. He rubbed his whisker-bristled mouth and rode downhill. By sundown, his walled tent was set up on the stream bank. From his gear he had put together the fishing rod and tied a delicate-looking feather on the hook.

This fly he danced on the water, causing several trout to rise for it, but none that he caught. Not disappointed, he worked downstream, enjoying the dimples and an occasional tussle with a cutthroat.

He looked up when she rode up on a painted pony and reined him to a halt on the edge of the water.

"Hello. Your sister said you were not with him anymore," Slocum said, busy watching the line's action in the current.

"Red Elk needs no woman."

"You know where there's some elk to eat this winter?"

"Yes, and I saw you coming."

"Oh," he said, missing another aggressive fish too. "What's that?" he asked when she held up a sack.

"Walnuts," she said and tossed them down. They clunked on the ground.

He laughed. She dismounted and ran to hug him. At the same moment, a large trout broke out of the water dancing on his tail. He reared back to set the hook and they both fell into the cold stream. Fighting the fish, splashing and laughing, they struggled to the bank.

"You're plain good luck, girl. Plain good luck."

Watch for

SLOCUM AND THE DESERTER

277th novel in the exciting SLOCUM series
from Jove

Coming in March!

J. R. ROBERTS
THE GUNSMITH

LONGARM

Explore the exciting Old West with one of the men who made it wild!